Distances

Conversation Pieces

A Small Paperback Series from Aqueduct Press

1. The Grand Conversation
   Essays by L. Timmel Duchamp

2. With Her Body
   Short Fiction by Nicola Griffith

3. Changeling
   A Novella by Nancy Jane Moore

4. Counting on Wildflowers
   An Entanglement by Kim Antieau

5. The Traveling Tide
   Short Fiction by Rosaleen Love

6. The Adventures of the Faithful Counselor
   A Narrative Poem by Anne Sheldon

7. Ordinary People
   A Collection by Eleanor Arnason

8. Writing the Other: A Practical Approach
   by Nisi Shawl & Cynthia Ward

9. Alien Bootlegger
   A Novella by Rebecca Ore

10. The Red Rose Rages (Bleeding)
    A Short Novel by L. Timmel Duchamp

11. Talking Back
    Epistolary Fantasies
    edited by L. Timmel Duchamp

12. Absolute Uncertainty
    Short Fiction by Lucy Sussex

13. Candle in a Bottle
    A Novella by Carolyn Ives Gilman

14. Knots
    Short Fiction by Wendy Walker

15. Naomi Mitchison: A Profile of Her Life and Work
    A Monograph by Lesley A. Hall

16. We, Robots
    A Novella by Sue Lange

17. Making Love in Madrid
    A Novella by Kimberly Todd Wade

18. Of Love and Other Monsters
    A Novella by Vandana Singh

19. Aliens of the Heart
    Short Fiction by Carolyn Ives Gilman

20. Voices From Fairyland:
    The Fantastical Poems of Mary Coleridge, Charlotte Mew, and Sylvia Townsend Warner
    Edited and With Poems by Theodora Goss

21. My Death
    A Novella by Lisa Tuttle

22. De Secretis Mulierum
    A Novella by L. Timmel Duchamp

23. Distances
    A Novella by Vandana Singh

24. Three Observations and a Dialogue:
    Round and About SF
    Essays by Sylvia Kelso and a correspondence with Lois McMaster Bujold

25. The Buonarotti Quartet
    Short Fiction by Gwyneth Jones

26. Slightly Behind and to the Left
    Four Stories & Three Drabbles
    by Claire Light

27. Through the Drowsy Dark
    Short Fiction and Poetry
    by Rachel Swirsky

28. Shotgun Lullabies
    Stories and Poems by Sheree Renée Thomas

29. A Brood of Foxes
    A Novella by Kristin Livdahl

About the Aqueduct Press Conversation Pieces Series

The feminist engaged with sf is passionately interested in challenging the way things are, passionately determined to understand how everything works. It is my constant sense of our feminist-sf present as a grand conversation that enables me to trace its existence into the past and from there see its trajectory extending into our future. A genealogy for feminist sf would not constitute a chart depicting direct lineages but would offer us an ever-shifting, fluid mosaic, the individual tiles of which we will probably only ever partially access. What could be more in the spirit of feminist sf than to conceptualize a genealogy that explicitly manifests our own communities across not only space but also time?

Aqueduct's small paperback series, Conversation Pieces, aims to both document and facilitate the "grand conversation." The Conversation Pieces series presents a wide variety of texts, including short fiction (which may not always be sf and may not necessarily even be feminist), essays, speeches, manifestoes, poetry, interviews, correspondence, and group discussions. Many of the texts are reprinted material, but some are new. The grand conversation reaches at least as far back as Mary Shelley and extends, in our speculations and visions, into the continually-created future. In Jonathan Goldberg's words, "To look forward to the history that will be, one must look at and retell the history that has been told." And that is what Conversation Pieces is all about.

L. Timmel Duchamp

Jonathan Goldberg, "The History That Will Be" in Louise Fradenburg and Carla Freccero, eds., *Premodern Sexualities* (New York and London: Routledge, 1996)

Published by Aqueduct Press
PO Box 95787
Seattle, WA 98145-2787
www.aqueductpress.com

This book is fiction. Names, characters, businesses, organizations, places, events, and incidents either are the product of the author's imagination or are used fictitiously. Any resemblance to actual persons, living or dead, events, or locales is entirely coincidental.

Copyright © 2008 by **Vandana Singh**
All rights reserved.
12 11 10   2 3 4 5

ISBN: 978-1-933500-26-3

Cover Design by Lynne Jensen Lampe
Book Design by Kathryn Wilham
Original Block Print of Mary Shelley by Justin Kempton:
www.writersmugs.com

Cover photo of Pleiades Star Cluster
NASA Hubble Telescope Images, STScI-2004-20
http://hubble.nasa.gov/image-gallery/astronomy-images.html
Credit: NASA, ESA, and AURA/Caltech
Front cover illustration by Thomas E. Duchamp

Printed in the USA by Applied Digital Imaging, Bellingham, WA

Acknowledgments

This story was written in my usual way: through the writing of a random sentence to find out where it led. That original first sentence is long lost but it led me farther afield, perhaps, than any other place I have been.

I would like to thank my husband Christopher for patiently wading through three drafts of the manuscript and for much-needed encouragement. My gratitude also goes out to my parents-in-law, Melanie and Russ, for their critical and enthusiastic reading of the manuscript. I am indebted to the members of the Cambridge Speculative Fiction Workshop for their intelligent and sometimes ruthless feedback on the second draft. In particular, I thank Jim Kelly for his invaluable comments on the second draft, and for generous encouragement.

I am deeply grateful for the enormous help I received from my publishers at Aqueduct. I thank Timmi Duchamp for immediately getting what my story was about, for helping me look deeper into it, and for her critical enthusiasm and support whenever I needed it. My thanks go out also to Kath Wilham for her patience and attention; specifically for her fine-tooth-comb reading of the text, the catching of little errors and inconsistencies, and for rendering the whole thing into its final, readable form. To Tom Duchamp I'm eternally obliged for a wonderful mini-crash-course on differential geometry, spread over several telephone conversations. I thank Tom for his generosity and insight. Any errors, omissions or misinterpretations (mathematical or otherwise) that might still lurk in the manuscript are, of course, entirely my responsibility.

For my sister-in-law, Ramaa,
with gratitude and affection.

Conversation Pieces
Volume 23

Distances

A Novella

by

Vandana Singh

Distances

Anasuya walked up the dim hallways of the Temple of Mathematical Arts toward the central atrium, her favorite place of repose. She had been three days in the amnion, and the abrupt return to physical reality always left her feeling disoriented and vaguely claustrophobic. The narrow stone passageways seemed to press in closer; the upward slope made her thighs ache. She felt the full weight of her body, slight though it was, as a new burden. For three days she had been soaring in multiple dimensions — now she was back to crawling across a two-d floor like a little desert roll-bug. But strangest of all was the solid presence of things, the way they were weighted by their physicality. Going up into the light, she had to touch the cold stone walls, pass her fingers over the carvings on the archways, brush the soft tapestries — as though to remember the world again.

But for now the world seemed too much with her, the walls too close. She fought the impulse to run — up the passageway, out of the Temple, into the hard light of the bone-dry City, the desertscape, the empty, waterless sky, where she pictured herself falling to her knees in the sand, the air seeping out of her lungs, the blood drying in her veins. She caught her breath, quickened her footsteps, passed under the frieze of the great god Anhutip and into the atrium.

Here her breathing grew easier. The atrium was the highest point of the hollowed-out mesa that housed the temple; its ceiling arched into a vast, soft darkness, below which mica windows let in the autumnal light. Above her the rays crossed each other, tilting imperceptibly with the movement of the sun. She walked among the tiers of light, the pools of light on the stone floor, among the stone sculptures and holographic illusions, until she reached the center of the atrium. From the ceiling above, which was lost in darkness, a long rope hung, bearing a complex, translucent sculpture in shards of colored glass. It moved slowly to and fro, driven by an invisible mechanism, dappling the atrium with a kaleidoscope of turquoise, mauve, and yellow light. Already she was feeling calmer. She sat down on the circular stone bench below the sculpture. There was a small, bubbling fountain in the space enclosed by the bench, from which she took a handful of glittering water that she splashed over her face and neck-slits. She looked into the tiny pool, where bristle-worms swam in the near-dark, all aglow, and felt the familiar comfort of their presence. She smoothed the thin shift she wore over her slender green body, stretched her legs, raised her arms above her head. As the light washed over her in great, slow waves, she was reminded, inevitably, of Sagara, the distant sea—the underwater caves and cliffs and seaweed forests of her childhood.

She lay in the shifting light, her thoughts wandering to this last session in the amnion. She had completed the task that had been assigned to her—it had taken a long time and a lot of tedious work, but it had been easy. She was beginning to fear that in just four years of exile she was already getting tired of things. Was it that she was coming to the end of something? Would she find that her life here, her mates, her work, had been some kind of mirage?

Her thoughts were interrupted by the arrival of the doorkeeper Amas, who moved through the columns of light and darkness like a nervous fish, his wide, brown face reverent. He held a bowl of steaming tea in one hand, while his other hand fumbled with a small holo. She took the tea.

"Do you know," Amas said in a conspiratorial whisper, "we have sky people visiting! The Master's been with them all afternoon."

Off-world tourists, she thought, probably from the moon-world of Sarakira, or the planet Charak, where there was a large mining colony. Or maybe they were from a trade-ship. Before she could ask what the Master was doing with them, he held out the holo to her, half-apologetically.

"Show me?"

"It is a dance of hyperbolas, Amas," she said gently. "See? Put your finger against the side, like this. In a moment the hyperbolas will morph. Watch with me."

It was the sort of mathematical art that the Temple gave to tourists and pilgrims—pretty, but with no subtlety. Amas—some called him Poor Amas, or Slow Amas—watched with awed, round eyes. "Oh," he said. She knew he didn't understand her explanations, but he liked to hear her say the words. He gave her a quick, shy, worshipful glance that made her sigh inwardly and left her to her solitude.

After he left she sipped the bitter tea, stretching her bare legs. The soliforms that gave her skin its green, exotic tint opened their microscopic petals to the light. She brushed her long black hair away from her neck and examined a tiny scattering of brown flecks on her shoulder. She had first noticed them four days ago. She thought about her mother Lata's body, Lata on the reed-raft that had been their home, Lata in the water, sunlight gleaming on her green skin, pointing out to the young Anasuya the mathematical harmonies of the world. Lata had been old then. I can't remember, she thought, whether Lata had brown spots on her body. As always, thinking about Lata made the old grief come alive again. Her hand shook; she set the bowl of tea beside her on the bench.

A senior acolyte passed by in a swirl of robes, ghost-like among the long rays of light, fractured momentarily by shadow and brightness.

"Have you heard," he said to her in passing, "we have off-worlders visiting. Not tourists—some kind of official delegation from Tirana! Traveled on a ship for eighteen years to get here. I wonder what they want."

Before she had time to make sense of this startling piece of news, they were upon her, the Master with the off-world visitors in tow. She stood up and made her salutation, palms crossed on chest. The strangers mimicked her, fumbling the simple gesture. There were eight of them, bare of face, with black, thick hair in elaborate coiffures. They wore bright tunics over close-fitting trousers and jewels hanging from their ears. Standing beside them, it was the Master who looked, at that moment, strange to her gaze, with the jade plate on his left cheek, flush with his brown skin, and a ruby cranial plate with ridges and pleats that glowed in the light.

"An official delegation of mathematicians from the Lattice of Tirana itself!" said the Master sibilantly. There were introductions, voices that echoed through the vast stone hall and were lost; she tried to shape her tongue around unfamiliar syllables, realizing with some incredulity that here were people more foreign than she, people from the stars! Kzoric: largeness, roundness, loud voice, spherical geometries on the outside, including the enormous round bun of hair, but her gaze was prickly, sawtooth. Vishk: small, thin, skulking in the shadows, parabolic stoop of back. Tall Hiroq: long face, almost an ellipse, almost bilateral symmetry, long hands fumbling shyly with a neck-clasp, voice deep and rich, quick, shy blinks, glance a sine wave — smooth, curious, and shy all at once. There were three others whose names she forgot, who remained standing at the back, deferentially. But the person who registered with her most was Nirx, who had an unconscious air of authority, for all she bowed and smiled and looked around with childish wonder. Nirx was small and compact, her hair in a braided bun of pleasing symmetry, her face old and wrinkled in complicated and interesting ways, like river mouths bifurcating, entering a sea. Her gaze was sharp, but with a kindness and a reserve. To Anasuya she was like a two-d projection of a multi-dimensional object—a lot was compressed into what she spoke, the way she looked at Anasuya. A woman of secrets, not immediately decipherable, Anasuya thought.

Nirx held in her hands a crystal bottle filled with an amber fluid.

"…Mathematician Nirx here," said the Master ponderously, lisping through his terrible teeth, "Mathematician Nirx has discovered a new sthanas—a new geometrical space! One that is complex beyond understanding! She has condensed the poetry of this space into a series of elegant equations. But so far these equations have not been solved, for they are intractable to an unexpected degree. Thus Mathematician Nirx and her team have traveled for years from the planet Tirana to see whether our mathematics can help them.

"It is only right that the Temple of Mathematical Arts, first Temple of Anhutip, who knows all forms and relations, should be chosen for this honor. On all of Sura, there is no place more sacred, more famous, for the solution of mathematical poems. And you… You are our best rider, Anasuya, for all that you are young. I offer you this…this poem, with the hope that you will accept."

The Master took the bottle of amber fluid from Nirx in his trembling, parchment-like hands and held it out to Anasuya. His humped, twisted body, with the bulbous nose and long-drawn-out face, cast grotesque shadows around him. Under the brilliant crimson skull, his shadowed eyes watched her. She had never been able to read the Master. He was like a carelessly assembled mess of contradictory geometries, all jagged, moody edginess and abrupt changes of behavior; his intensity alternated with apathy and aloofness. But she forgot him as she took the bottle in her hands.

What new sthanas was this? What undiscovered mathematical country lay within?

She felt an anticipatory tingle of excitement. Maybe this was just what she needed.

"I am honored to accept," she said at last.

"We admire greatly your analog methods of computation," the Tirani woman Nirx said in a little, piping voice. She spoke the language without hesitation but with a lilting accent that was quite foreign. Her hands fluttered like insects, a pleasing harmony. "We have heard about it from travelers and traders and old records from earlier visitors to Sura. With our scant knowledge of your techniques, we constructed molecules whose interactions mimic the behavior of the new equations. But our reaction vats are crude compared to yours! Nor are the molecules very stable, being tremendously complex—so we must reconfigure the solution every few days from the seed…"

Each mathematical poem had its secret, inner space, its universe, nestled within its equations the way meaning was enclosed by words. That inner space or solution space — the sthanas — was the poem's regime of validity, the place where the poem came true. Holding the bottle up to the rays of light, Anasuya felt the familiar mixture of anticipation and exhilaration — and a curious switching of realities, as though the external world of people and lovers, the weight of her own incompleteness, her hopeless, endless nostalgia, had lost all definition, and the abstractions of mathematics were once again the things of true substance, tangible, real.

She was a rider like no other. Her function was to lie in an amnion that had been specially constructed for her, with her neck-slits open. The sap that was exuded by the feathery organs inside her neck-slits and by the undersides of her fingernails and the tips of her breasts — the sap her people called *vapasjal*, that which is given back or returned — contained microscopic organelles the chemists at the temple called spiroforms. The spiroforms tasted the molecules in the mixture; as they interacted with the chemical stew of the amnion, a space blossomed in her mind, the most abstract made-world there could be: the sthanas itself: the solution-space of the mathematics. The tiny, invisible machines that swam in the fluid recorded the chemical changes wrought by the spiroforms and transmitted to the Temple's data banks a holographic representation of this inner space, brick by proverbial brick. Other holo-riders had to sit directly in front of a display that recorded the chemical reactions in the standard vats, and, through a complex science of interpretation and analysis, including trial and error and constant tinkering, they had to attempt to fill in the solution space of the given mathematics. For Anasuya this process was like a blind person mapping the contours of the world with a stick, and it horrified her because for her mathematics was experiential, a sixth sense that bared before her the harmonies, natural and artificial, that formed the sub-text of the world. Floating in the amnion, she entered unmapped territory; she was a speck, a ship lost in vastness, a rider on waves of maxima and minima, an explorer of a space that, but for her, would remain only guessed at. She entered this mathematical country as an explorer would enter a new land: she looked for singularities, skated over manifolds, sketched out the abstract, mountainous terrain of bizarre mathematical functions; she sought branch points and branch cuts and hidden territories bearing algebraic surprises. She took the esoteric world of the sthanas and made it her reality.

The molecules that Mathematician Nirx had brought gave her dream-like glimpses of a deep, cerulean darkness, fraught with hints of strange regularities, punctuated by fine silver lines and complexly looping tangles. This mathematical country lay spread in several dimensions; she would have to visualize it slice by three-dimensional slice. During the preliminary session she explored, soaring and swooping, tasting this new sthanas. It was beautiful, beautiful! This would take days…months, maybe a lifetime! Even at low molecular concentrations, which blurred details, she could sense shadowy structures pricking out of the darkness. There were layers and layers here, patterns that promised to be astonishing. Exploring this sthanas gave her a rush that was better than anything she had experienced in a long time. This was what it was like to be in the great saltwater marshes of the home she had left behind—to taste the richness and complexity of the universe through this most astonishing of senses—this was what it was like to be Anasuya.

After the preliminary session she scrubbed distractedly in the shower and let herself be subjected to the ministrations of the temple chemists, who pronounced her free of toxic remnants and the brew safe for further study. They handed her a tall glass of thick protein shake, which she drank down in a few gulps. She emerged still shaken with the wonder of it all.

There was a flurry of activity in the analysis room. The Tiranis and temple chemists were already working on reconfiguring the molecules. A holo showed a real-time image of what Anasuya had seen. Anasuya sat down before it, acknowledging the greetings of her colleagues. It was a good replica for an initial survey, needing only a few edits. "Every analogy has its limits," she remembered her old teacher Bakul telling her, when Anasuya first started her studies at the Temple. "The analogy is to the true mathematics what your shadow is to you. So after the work is done, you must study the holo and employ the art of mathegraphia—rebuild the sthanas—look for errors, artifacts, places where the information is incomplete. Use your mathematical knowledge to fill in the gaps!"

Bakul was dead now, but her student remembered. An initial coarse-grain survey of the solution-space was unlikely to have major detectable errors, if the chemistry was any good. Anasuya made the few edits needed and got up. She looked at the great stone bulk of the amnion, with the data pipes snaking from it, and the fat chemical feed tubes and breathing apparatus…and suppressed a sigh of longing. Turning away, she caught the eye of the old Tirani woman, Mathematician Nirx.

"We sent you to a strange place, I think," Nirx said, smiling. She had an oddly penetrating gaze. "It will take us perhaps two days to reconfigure the mixture and make some adjustments to your…what do you call them? Micro-machines? We will be using solutions of greater concentration so that you can see more details. Then we proceed, yes?"

Anasuya nodded, smiled. And thought to herself: two days! How was she going to wait that long?

She went up to the atrium, all her old restlessness displaced by the excitement of this new project. Draping herself by the little central pool, she took a few deep breaths, leaned over to look into the water. The bristle-worms blinked messages at each other in rapid light-flashes, as though mimicking her hastened breath, her new exhilaration.

Suddenly a shadow fell across her, and the water was tinged faintly red. She turned, startled.

The Master stood before her, made monstrous in the ever-changing light, his crimson cranial plate aglow.

"These Tirani strangers," he said in his harsh lisp, speaking low, bending toward her so she shrank back a little. His metallic, fringed teeth moved sibilantly over each other. "This Nirxian poetry, these new equations. I do not trust them. Nobody but Anhutip could breathe such a sthanas into being—it is too complex! It must represent something, some physical system we have yet to discover. A highly sophisticated machine, or an alien being of great complexity—who can tell? I want you to find out what it is. What use it could be put to. Don't tell anyone but me. Will you? Will you do this, Anasuya?"

Anasuya had also wondered whether this sthanas of Nirx was the representation of some physical system. But correspondences to reality, or what others narrowly defined to be reality, were less important to her than the mathematics—and the uses of things were not even of peripheral concern. She opened her mouth to argue this, realized the futility of it, and instead nodded her agreement. He was the Master after all. She was discomfited by him now as much as she had been when she first came here.

After he left she remembered how it had been for her, meeting him the first time. He was, like her, from another place, already bent and old and ugly when he came. Even after years in the City, his speech was guttural, betraying his origins in Ifara, on the other side of the planet. He had smiled tentatively at Anasuya the first time they met, and she had nearly screamed when she saw his teeth. There were two small humps on his shoulder blades, and it was said that he was a genetic splice of the great winged gwi, a deep-desert sapient-worm, and a human, although nobody had seen any evidence of wings or fins. Everyone knew that in Ifara the soulless witch-folk performed horrible genetic mutilations as part of their religious customs. She knew she should feel sorry for him, but he disturbed her too much, even for that. What kind of thing was he, not human, not gwi, not worm, but a bit of each? At least she knew what she was...

So when first he tried to take her under his wing (so to speak), mumbling eagerly about her amazing natural talent and how he would hone it and train it into something pure and beautiful, she was frightened and a little horrified. Fortunately it was easy to find other teachers. In any case, the Master was too old for real work. In his autumnal years he dabbled in mathematical art and let the temple high directorate do the work of running the place. His art was on exhibit in the public halls of the temple; there was an exhibit even here, in the atrium. All his work was minimalist, strange, consisting of representations of mathematical functions floating in a white space. Operators fluttered through this space, and as they grazed past the functions they transformed them, introducing discontinuities and reducing their domains of definition. After some iterations nothing but the white space was left, whereupon the initial configuration reappeared and the cycle began again. The City's critics called the effect meditative, transcendental, but to Anasuya the holos were horrifyingly sad. She avoided them much as she avoided the Master.

She got up. The Master had disturbed her mood of elation, breaking it up as certainly as one of his little function-destroying operators. Making a mental note to avoid him over the next few days, she walked quickly to the great temple doors. Perhaps she should go home to her mates, whom she hadn't seen now for four days. At the door she turned around to see the little doorkeeper come running, holding her gray cloak that she had forgotten. He was out of breath, his broad, bare face crumpled with concern. "Forgetting your cloak. Evenings are cold," Amas said, arranging the soft folds around her shoulders, reaching up to do so, stepping back in confusion because he had dared touch her skin. She knew he wanted to hear all about her day and the wonders she had seen. "They say it is the most important, the hardest poem ever," he said in awe. "And you'll solve it." She smiled, moved despite herself. "I'm tired, Amas. I'll tell you all about it later."

She stepped outside into coolness and a red sky. The sun was setting behind the mesas; the first stars were out. Around her the city had come alive, as it did every evening, surprising her even now—tiers of lit windows in every mesa, every made-house, the walkways and speeder stations aglow, crowded with citizens. A broad flight of steps led from the ornate pillars of the

Temple to the plaza below. On the roof behind her, the god Anhutip's giant image perched, his ruby eyes burning. She stood in the deep pool of his shadow, halted by a familiar hesitancy.

She had never gotten used to the great stone city. She had traveled on its walkways, wandered between towers of granite and red sandstone, gone to the tellings at the public temples on every festival day; she had admired the stark beauty of the arid gardens with their wind-sculpted rock formations and the stone fountains in every plaza from which flowed—not water, but light, a marvelous illusion wrought by technology. On the sides of mesas and made-houses, waves of light flowed like water over the pebbly bed of a stream, illuminating mica and feldspar and quartz buried in the stone. The citizens went about their business as though unaware of the beauty of their environs—they wore loose, flowing clothes, gemplates on their faces and scalps, and their skin was brown, not green like Anasuya's. The City had made her welcome; she even had a proper House to belong to, and companionship and intimacy, instead of the crowded anonymity of a Temple common-house where she had first lived after she left home. Her House was a pentad: she had the love of four people when some had none. She didn't know why, despite all this, she felt like a stranger here, after all these years. Perhaps it was simply that the spiroforms sang in her blood, locked in symbiosis with the soliforms that greened her skin and marked her always a foreigner: a woman from the remote edge of the continent where saltwater marshes bred a folk stranger than the humans from other worlds.

But also there was an alien quality to everything here: the air was thin and dry, the stars seemed bright and close in the cold nights. The vastness of the sky was overpowering. The city itself was an artifice; other than the hollowed-out mesas and the stone building materials, everything here was made by human hands or their proxies. There were few animals besides the small desert crustaceans, the roll-bugs and flying stingers, and the wide-ranging gwi, the intelligent, winged reptilian creatures of the high mountains, seen rarely outside the migratory season. When they cried in their strange, harsh voices, Anasuya felt an answering, inexplicable sorrow.

Only twice a year, when the City played host to two great migratory gatherings that had (in some forgotten past) birthed the original habitation that was to become the City—only then did the character of the City change. The severity of the mesas and made-houses was softened somewhat by the skin-tents of the peri-humans, the roosts of the gwi atop the mesas. Then the streets filled with strange beasts, exotic music and languages, and there were trade-stops on every corner and, if needed, new wells were dug into the great underground aquifer that made life possible in this barren place. As was appropriate for visiting deities, the guest gods were taken in processions to meet the old gods of the desert, Anhutip and the Two Lovers, Ekatip and Shunyatip, and there was much feasting, badinage, and material exchange between their respective followers. Those who wished to lie with followers of the strange gods went to the Temple of the Two Lovers, where few things were taboo. There, under the stone images of Ekatip and Shunyatip, who always sat back to back, facing away from each other and gazing into time in opposite directions, the priests ladled out festival stews, blessed the couplings, and comforted the lonely. It was there that Anasuya had stayed when she first came to the City. Even the followers of Anhutip were welcome at the Temple of the Two Lovers, despite the fact that Anhutip was the one who had played a trick on the two gods, sundering them in time, and stealing from them all knowledge of Number. Anhutip the Mathematician, the mischief maker, who had breathed the world into being. There were elaborate dramas and street shows in the plazas commemorating the old stories. The scant desert rain fell at this time, too, filling the air with the moist aroma of memory: the desert remembering water. These were the only times that Anasuya felt as though something in her was coming alive, unfolding petal by petal.

But now she stood outside the great, closed doors of Anhutip's Temple, looking down into a cascade of lit stone steps, thinking she couldn't go home after all. Not just yet. She couldn't bear the long trip over the walkways, the presence of other citizens so secure in their belonging to this place, so nonchalant in their happiness. Like her mates... She had not seen them for four days—another two or three days would surely not matter. Besides, she had the new sthanas to wait for...

She sighed. There was a faint haze over the city, which always caused a certain odor to hang in the air: a smell of stone and metal, the invisible effervescence of the machinery that smoothly and silently underlay the city. She found the smell vaguely disturbing; it emphasized to her the absence of water. It rained here only about twice a year, and each time the brief rain was like a mockery of the endless bounty of the sea.

The first time that the harmonies of the world became clear to her, she was in her fifth year. Her birth-mother and other mothers had been anxious for her, muttering to each other when they thought she was not listening. "The child, Anasuya," they said, "will she ever be gifted by the sea? Or will she be forgotten?" But the gift—what her people called *athmis*—was in her, waiting.

Growing up on the sloping beaches of Sagara—amid the phallic pneumetaphores of the marshgrove trees, on the slippery, matted floors of the raft-islands—swimming in the green, dappled light of the seaweed forest, she had always suspected that there were hidden patterns underlying the variegated splendor of the world. The athmis came alive in her while she was swimming underwater between rafts on a perfect, ordinary day. Years later she could recall it with clarity: the feel of salt water in her mouth and neck-slits, a singing in her veins that made her prickle all over, and the new sense awakening inside her like a window opening in a blank wall. Then the sudden crescendo of mathematical harmonies in her mind, as she floated in the marsh forest: in the fractal landscape, a shimmering of sinusoidal disturbances as an eel swam by, the delicate exponentiation evident in parthenogenic two-fish birthing in the water, each daughter fish budding off two more daughters before swimming away. Gazing at ripples cross each other in ever expanding circles, she realized with a rush of delight that the book of knowledge had opened to her, revealing the secret relationships between things: the length and undulation of waves and their speed, the height of a falling rock and the time it took to splash into the sea. The myriad geometries surrounding her became readily apparent: the smooth swell of the waves, the hollows between them, the dimpling of tiny whirlpools as the water swept between the weeds. She had no names yet for so many things, but she sensed the mathematics of the world as a young child knows colors before it learns the words. The realization swept over her that everything in the world was in constant conversation with every other thing, that all was flux and play. Swimming in the green and gold light, she knew she would never be alone in such a world.

Going back to her mothers, rendered nearly speechless by excitement, she had looked for a way to tell them what she had come to understand. One of her mothers had picked her up, saying: Little Fish, what are you trying to say? And she had found her voice in her first mathematical poem.

> Fish!
> Fish fish!
> Fish fish fish fish!

And the women had laughed in delight. But Lata put her face close to the child's and looked gently into Anasuya's eyes.

"What happens after all those fish?"

Anasuya, recovering breath, said

"More fish!"

"Child, if your poem were true, not just Sagara but all the world would be running over with fish!"

Anasuya's eyes filled with tears. Had she spoken a false poem?

"Your poem is true," Lata said, wiping her tears, hoisting her up on a broad hip and walking away over the beach. "But it is only a small part of a greater truth. The world is not over-run by fish because there are other things in the world than fish! The big fish that eat the little ones. The seasons when the water turns too cold or too warm. How many kiputi pods are in the water. So know this: that no poem we can speak is ever a complete poem. No truth we can utter is ever a complete truth. Everything is what it is because of other things as well as its own nature. So there is no thing removed from other things. Thus you are Anasuya, but you are also the sea, and the fish, and the athmis that is in us all. Remember this! Thus we end all poems with the phrase: My poem is incomplete!"

Days later Anasuya lay floating in the green water, idly watching darters swoop in the translucent depths below. Then a poem more true than the first one came to her.

> Fish
> Fish fish
> Fish fish fish fish
> Fish fish fish fish fish fish fish fish
> Big Fish!
> My poem is incomplete!

Her mothers were grateful that the sight Anasuya had been gifted with was both beautiful and harmless—and relatively common among their people. There were others whose gift was less benevolent; there were people who could sense the dreams of others, or see alternate worlds that defied logic and common sense. There were one or two every year who came to understand, with the flowering of their athmis, the language of those ponderous creatures, the seaphants; these children would leave their homes with a seaphant pod, ranging up and down the coast, coming home once a year after the season of the rains. But in that time they would have become more seaphant than human, losing knowledge of their own language and unable to communicate fluently with their own mothers. And once there was a young boy who turned inward, became mute, his eyes gone blank and opaque, seeing something nobody else could see. Once every few years the light would return to his eyes, and he would speak the words of some unknown tongue. So the gift was not always kind. But in some unfathomable way all forms of the gift were necessary, her mothers told her. The gift was part of the great circle of living and dying, giving and receiving.

In her fifteenth year Anasuya joined, for the first time, the women in the skin tents; she learnt the use of herbs to prevent or enable pregnancy, and she learnt to anticipate the long boats of the Sunset Clan men, as they came swiftly, urgently over the water. She came to know the men by their individual geometries, their particular graces of speech and movement, the delicacy with which one touched her, the dark pools of another's eyes. She learned the language of bodies, men with women, women with women, joining and coming apart. But most of all she learned the young man whose name was Hasha.

He had long limbs, and his eyes were as green as his skin, and he did not braid his black hair but let it fly about his face. The athmis was strong in him, but the visions it brought him made no sense to him or anyone else, however grand and strange they seemed to be. He liked to tell Anasuya about the things he saw: great, gleaming structures moving through emptiness, filled with people as a pod is with seeds; gold-colored oceans that did not move, upon which tiny people crawled, erecting massive structures of stone. There was a restlessness about Hasha that disturbed and excited her. He wanted to roam the world and find the places he saw in his visions, even though the elders said those places didn't exist except in his mind. Don't let the Trickster take you, boy, they said. To leave, to step out of the circle—that is not the way of the children of the sea. But Hasha couldn't stop dreaming of what lay beyond the known world. The two of them would lie in one of the numerous hollows made by the roots of wind trees, where they were sheltered from the wild whipping of the broad, wing-like leaves, and there they would talk and make love.

Later that year Anasuya left the leafy canopies of her mothers' home and went with Lata to live on a raft above the seaweed forest so that she might better learn the use of her gift. Life with Lata was early rising into pink dawns, the taste of fresh-caught fish, the slippery feel of the reed-mats under her bare feet, and the teaching, learning, and classification of harmonies, their secret inter-relationships, the means by which they gave order and beauty to the world. Anasuya had already learned some of the words that enabled her to describe mathematical relationships; now she learned the language in greater depth and more formality, learning to weave concepts into songs. She learned the art of rendering abstractions into visual symbols drawn on wet sand with a finger—spirals, circles, lines wavy and straight, fraught with meaning. She sang with Lata, their voices rising over the constant wash of waves, the sound of the wind, and the raucous cries of the flying fish.

Their reed island swayed and floated lazily over the seaweed forest, anchored by a tether made of fish-antennae. At night they watched the two moons follow each other across the sky, and Anasuya understood with a shock of joy that the harmonies she sought existed not only in the sea but everywhere, expressed in the precise orbits of the moons, the wheeling of the distant stars.

> Raindrops on still water.
> Circles, ever expanding.
> Only the Great Proportion
> Stays the same.
> If the circle were to spread
> Across Sea and Earth and Sky
> Would the Great Proportion remain?
> It remains the same and yet
> It contains infinity...
> My poem is incomplete.

It was Lata who told her about other peoples, other worlds, thus confirming Hasha's visions. People of stone living in oceans of sand; star-people making their way from world to world in the sea of the sky. And from Lata Anasuya heard again the familiar stories of childhood: the Trickster Wave and the Three Women, the Cave of Delusion, stories about the seaphants, the leviathans...

"Tell me about the leviathans."

Distances

Years later Anasuya would remember what it was like: lying beneath a sky full of stars, the water aglitter with moonlight, the squeaking of wet reeds rubbing against one another as the swells gently rocked the raft, the faint, pungent smell of fish drying across the doorway of the reed cabin. Lata's voice in the darkness.

"What the leviathans are, nobody knows, but there are stories about them. You can tell a fish by the shape of the water that closes around it as it swims. All we are is impressions on the water, ripples in the sea. All we are — circles, feedback loops, cycles of the seasons, of being and becoming. The leviathans were once travelers in the seas of the sky, and there are stories about how they came to fall into this sea. Some stories say that they were struck by lightning from the stars and thus fell, and becoming immobile, learned to live at the bottom of the sea, spawning the sea-people among other living beings, becoming takers and givers of life. Other stories say that the leviathans, in their journeys across the starry reaches of the sky, were pursued by Darkness and Light and found escape here in the warm waters of this ocean, our Sagara. In these stories the leviathans were not all of one kind; the elders, who were a slow, gravid species, wished only to spend their lives in endless contemplation. The young, of various species, wanted to go out into the world, to seed it, to explore. So the younger species left and populated the sea, but they did not forget the old ones, who still dream on the ocean bed, who need them and give back to them even as they lie like great, drowned islands, their wide mouths sea-weed fringed, ever open, like caves. Yet other tales tell the opposite: that the humans were the ones who crashed into these waters from the sky, and the sea creatures, like the seaphants, came to them and aided them. But the humans had no athmis in them. So the sea creatures mated with them and gave them the athmis, and in return the humans gave them their abandoned sky vessels, which lay at the bottom of the ocean like a small mountain range, forming the reef we know today. The reef became a place of shelter for the great beings of the waters. In time the great beings lost their need of the open sea and grew large and heavy, and felt no need to go out of their shelter. The sea creatures of the open fed them with their own bodies when their bodies were of no use to them (as we do even now) and in their slow dreaming the leviathans did not forget the green sperm, the athmis, which they released into the water as a gift, as the vapasjal, that which is returned. As is the sap of the people of the sea also called vapasjal, because that, too, is returned to the sea and returns to the person so that in its signatures the person may read the sea's tongue and take part in its endless conversation."

Anasuya, listening sleepily, knew the sea was within her, as she was in the sea's embrace. Perhaps one day Hasha would understand too, that like her, he was part of the great system of interlocking circles. She thought of his restlessness and couldn't connect with it. In that moment of contentment she knew she would never leave.

Anasuya lay in the amnion, floating like a cloud over a new country. The environment of the amnion magnified her mathematical sense: the spiroforms went forth from her body like deep space probes from a mother ship, made their discoveries, and returned to her with the information, repeating the dance in a series of feedback loops that intensified the experience, so that after the first few minutes of immersion all her senses were attuned to this one, special sense, and she was lost to it, hopelessly, willingly.

Here was the new sthanas, rendered in greater detail than she had seen before. She was immersed in feathery complexity: the strange, geometrical vistas, the coils and loops of the space itself. She was swooping over a vast landscape, skimming dense tensor fields, familiarizing herself with its geometric structures, sensing the dynamical processes implicit in the Nirxian equations.

How to begin to understand this sthanas?

"When you want to know something that is as yet beyond your knowing," Lata had told her in the old days, "don't seek it the way a darter hones in on its prey. Empty your mind of all longing for result, conclusion, or reward. Play with the thing you wish to understand, swim in it, become part of it, and the answer will fall into your mind as surely as the kiputi pods fall into the water every spring."

So Anasuya let her mind go slack and gave herself up to the pleasures of this mathematical space, as she had once delighted in the intricate world of the seaweed forest. Running through the sthanas were the fine silver lines she had seen before, like threads from a great loom, falling and rising in complicated tangles. She followed one of the silver lines for a while, but was soon distracted by other structures. Mosaics pricked out of the darkness, and here and there were whorls and vortices, like mouths. She dived into one opening and found herself falling toward a vast plain of negative curvature. As she came closer she found that again hints of locally complex structure were making themselves apparent: leaf-like tessellations and lacy mosaics, and more vortices. She couldn't tell if the vortex she had dived into had spat her back to her starting point or whether she was seeing structure at a different scale. She wandered like a tourist, gazing, exulting. Here was the high rise of a cliff; following it she found herself at the lip of an overhang, and above and below her were great voids. Across the gap was the edge of another cliff. Glancing "down" she found that the cliff base was lost to sight and that the darkness seemed again to have faint hints of complex geometries.

Although she had been in the amnion nearly a whole day, it seemed hardly any time before she sensed that the molecules in the fluid were dissociating, because the images in her mind were dissolving, curling up at the edges, folding into themselves, the patterns giving way to chaos. She wanted to stop it—there was so much more to explore—but there was no going back until the next time.

As the sthanas broke up she saw its intricate geometries morph abruptly into a human face. A woman with brown skin and silver hair running off her head in fine lines — a stranger — looking at her across some unfathomable barrier. Although she existed for no more than a fraction of a second, there was nothing indistinct about her. She seemed to burn the space around her with her being. And then she was gone.

Sometimes, coming out of a solution-space, Anasuya would see strange residual forms and structures that had nothing to do with the problem at hand, but these illusions were usually abstract in nature. In part they were a result of the tendency of the human mind to perceive patterns even where patterns didn't exist. She had never seen a human face here before, let alone one so distinct that she could say with certainty that she didn't recognize it. She couldn't explain it as an image from her own memories.

She knew that as some chaotic systems evolved, they were interspersed with flashes of order — regular structures that appeared for certain values of the right parameter and then disappeared — but this felt different. The woman's face was so clear, her expression so urgent, as though she had a message for Anasuya, and Anasuya alone — that all explanations felt inadequate. And yet there was a familiarity about the woman, a familiarity about the feeling inside Anasuya that the experience had evoked. She would have to think about that later, when she was alone.

Shaking with excitement, she finished her shower and went to sit before the holo where her explorations had been recorded. The temple chemists and the Tiranis were cheering. Not a bad replica; she made a few minor edits and waited for the end of the recording to see if the strange woman's face would appear. But there was nothing there except the chaos of the space breaking up as the molecules dissociated.

"Next session in two days," one of the Temple chemists said, smiling at her. The reconfiguration process was already underway. Anasuya waved her goodbyes and left the analysis room.

As she went up the passageways of the Temple, Anasuya felt haunted by the image she had seen. Was it possible that the image of the woman was something to do with the physical system that this mathematics inevitably represented? Was this physical system the biology of a person, an alien? Yet she couldn't relate this hypothesis to the hazy feeling of familiarity that the image had evoked in her. It wasn't that she knew this woman, she decided, it was more that the woman seemed to represent something Anasuya knew. Her restlessness, her fears of always being a stranger here, her memories of home… Could it be that the image had been within her for a long time, hidden in her own mind, a secret door as yet unopened? Was it conceivable that the appearance of the woman had nothing to do with the nature of the mathematical space of Nirx's equations—that this new sthanas, being staggeringly complex, merely provided a means for this image to come into being?

But the thought also came to her that she would not know this for certain until she knew what physical system the new sthanas represented. She had no doubt now that the sthanas reflected some kind of reality. The look Nirx had given her after she emerged from the amnion—she remembered it now. Appreciation, mingled with some kind of sorrow or reluctance. And that reserve.

The Master, she had to admit, was right.

As though the thought had conjured him up, there was the Master, waiting for her. He was standing just before the great temple doors, blocking any possibility of escape. She stopped. He came to her, eagerly, anxiously.

"What do you think? What is it that the sthanas describes?"

She stepped back.

"It's too early to tell, Master," she said, hoping her annoyance didn't show on her face. "I suspect that it is a seven-dimensional space. I know nothing of its finer topological invariants, or its geometry. Please, give me time."

He hung his head. Over his face plate his eyes looked at her sadly. Abruptly he barked "Time!" His face changed in one of his disturbingly quick changes of mood. He grinned ferociously at her, turned on his heel, and left her as suddenly as he had come.

She spent the next two days in a misery of waiting, haunting the Temple atrium like a little fish in light and shadow, spending hours sipping a drink in the refectory, where a latticed rock wall let in the golden light of the desert.

Waiting, she had the ghost of an idea. She pushed it to the back of her mind. She knew better than to prod an idea before it was formed.

When the amnion became ready for her again, she concentrated on charting and mapping, attempting to confirm that the sthanas had seven dimensions. She had suspected, from her very first immersion, that the sthanas was non-trivial both in terms of its global topology and its local geometry; that everything about it would harbor surprises. Her first explorations had given her a feel for the space; now she concentrated on the tedious but necessary detail-work. Without this sort of rigor and method, there would be no basis, no foundation for wild flights of intuition. "Intuition," Batul had said, drawing up her eyebrows severely, "must be founded on what has been learned by method and practice. Otherwise the result is as likely to be nonsense as anything else."

While working she discovered that there were gaps in the sthanas, little, black, empty sections. They were few and far between, but puzzling. Effects like these were usually a result of bad chemistry. But she knew that the Temple chemists assigned to this project were the best ones. It was incomprehensible. Anasuya noted these sad, empty regions for future reference and continued her work.

Just as she had relegated her ghost of an idea to the back of her mind, she had also pushed away all conscious thought of the woman whose face she had seen in the last session. Only when the molecules of the brew started dissociating and the distinct topography of the space was whipped slowly into chaos did she start looking, half afraid that the face would not appear. But it was there.

The woman was looking at her and speaking, but Anasuya could not hear her words. There was a terrible urgency about the stranger. She gestured with her hands, in a way that reminded Anasuya of drawing figures in wet sand as a child. Her hair streamed out in silver lines that tangled in complex ways around her head. Her eyes were lined with wrinkles, her mouth opening and closing around words Anasuya could not hear. The words fell between Anasuya's fingers and were lost. They fell into her ear like a stone into a well, and she caught them just as the woman began to break up, her silver hair pulling apart from her head, spreading out, breaking up.

Art. Make art.

Again, an urgent whisper in the ear of her mind. *Make art.*

Memories came flooding. A shore, sloping down to the sea. Children drawing circles in wet sand. Gathering together mud, sand, pebbles, making sand people or mud people, shaping fish and seaphants. Standing up with the other children, holding a small sister or brother on her hip. Watching the tide wash it all away.

Later: the place of the ancestors. She was swimming there as a child, and one of her mothers was pointing out the artwork on the high cliff walls. The stories and poetry and mathematics of her people. She was struck by the notion that you could invest meaning in marks made on stone or sand. That it was possible to make beauty in this world as well as to discover it.

That had been before the athmis came alive in her.

When she went back to the place of the ancestors much later, the artwork was so stunning to her newly opened senses that she had to catch her breath and close her eyes. Opening them again, she had cried and laughed in delight.

In her years of apprenticeship at the Temple, she had learned the basic techniques of mathematical art. Learning to make beauty in the language of the god Anhutip was a sacred duty here, whether one intended to be an acolyte, a chemist, or a rider. She had to read and memorize the sixty-three commentaries on form and beauty. And later she had to learn how to make her own art holos. "It's all about how Anhutip walks in space and time," her instructor, the plump, genial Sozi had told her. "You have to think of form and balance dynamically, my dear. The evolution of the functions, the furling and unfurling in time—and what echo they leave in the still-unguessed mathematics of the emotions…" Sozi had made her impatient with his eloquence and his love of explanation, and the way his plump hands gestured. She was Anasuya, she could see the mathematics of the world directly, she knew exactly what he meant the first time. But when it came to doing the work, she found it challenging. Her imagination seemed to run up against a brick wall. She found that the ability to see and discover beauty was not equivalent to the ability to create it. "You are very young, my dear," said fat Sozi to her, sucking at his gourd-straw while his free hand described elegant harmonies in the air. "Be patient! It is not enough to see with those fabulous eyes of yours—you must conceptualize something that is your own. Breathe life into it as Anhutip did at the beginning of the world."

She had been angry and humiliated at first; she worked at mathematical art in a fury until Sozi finally pronounced to her that she had learned something. "Not bad," he had said, picking up one of her small holos. She was left with the dissatisfied, unsettled feeling that she had never mastered the art of making art, only become tolerably competent in it.

But mathematical art had never been her true love. Her true country, her only country now, was the sthanas, the solution space of mathematical equations, where she could ride and fly. So why was it that a stranger should come out of the chaos and tell her: make art?

Anasuya emerged from the amnion and scrubbed quickly in the shower, feeling puzzled and a little disappointed. Was that all the mysterious woman had to say? She didn't know what she had been expecting, but she had felt it would be something personal, some revelation about her life, her future: a promise, a freedom. But already there were people waiting for her, with towels and a fresh shift. She would have to think about this later.

In the analysis room she made an enormous effort to concentrate on the task at hand. She sat before the holo as the images rolled, pointing out interesting features to Nirx, as well as those puzzling regions of black space. These were different from the imperfections she had come across before—the defects that indicated the gap between the "reality" of Nirx's equations and their molecular analogs. "They are like little blind spots," Anasuya said. "I don't understand it. Perhaps the micros need to be checked."

But the Temple chemist Ahran, who was responsible for maintaining the micro-machines, indignantly denied that there was anything wrong with them.

"You know well, Anasuya, how careful we are with the micros. We test them ten times before we run the amnion."

Nirx's fingers fluttered in the now familiar gesture. She said placatingly:

"It is of no matter. We are finding out much, despite this."

While Anasuya made the edits she realized that what she did with the holo after each session was rather like art. To understand how to make a join or cut, one had to make choices that were, at their core, aesthetic in nature. What symmetries did the surfaces have that would enable them to be fully mapped? What did her intuition tell her about completing patterns, guessing a trend? In a sense, art would be an inverse operation — to construct, not deconstruct. To synthesize, not analyze. Yes, she would have to think about it.

Over the next few amnion sessions she dutifully continued charting the space, confirming, to the delight of the Tirani scientists, that the sthanas was indeed a seven-dimensional, differentiable manifold, homeomorphic to a seven-dimensional sphere, but with an exotic differentiable structure. There was a four-d subspace, a manifold immersed in the sthanas like a drowned country. Nirx seemed very interested in this subspace. She asked Anasuya to determine its metric, which was the clue to the curvature of this space, among other things. This Anasuya did, and found that it was a simple $(1,1,1,-1)$ metric belonging to a well-known category. The metric, however, was the simplest thing about the manifold. In the higher dimensional sthanas, this four-dimensional manifold twisted and looped dizzyingly, intersecting itself at various points like the knotted intestines of a great beast. The silver lines she had discovered in her first explorations were, in fact, these intersections. Nirx was enormously pleased with this discovery.

Meanwhile, the idea ghost that had come to Anasuya earlier was still in her mind, waiting to be formed more fully. And the woman's face appeared in the amnion now with clockwork regularity each time the molecules in the brew began to dissociate. The face was not young; the lines on it mathematical, beautiful, etched by pain and years. The eyes were large and haunting, filled with the now familiar urgency. In their burning gaze was the understanding of who Anasuya was and how she needed to be in this world. Each time her coming brought to Anasuya an inexplicable joy, a comforting familiarity. She breathed questions.

What is your name?

The answer was a stream that came out of the image's mouth. A sound Anasuya could not recall.

I'll call you Vara, she said. *Vara*, in her language, meant "ripple."

Tell me, Vara, where have you come from? What have you suffered?

Nothing but that long, slow look. The mouth remained closed on the answer.

What art should I do? What is the art a key to?

Words fell out of Vara's mouth, but Anasuya couldn't catch them. She had a vision, though, for a fraction of a second: she was standing before a blank white space, color oozing from her fingertips. There was something coming into being in that white space. She had one glimpse of it: a work of art of such staggering beauty and complexity that it seemed to simultaneously contain the world and be contained by it. And in it, like a ghost or a guide, was the image of Vara, her silver hair streaming.

Later Anasuya could not be sure she had seen what she thought she had seen—surely she had imagined that breathtaking vista. But whatever the source, it was there in her mind, an elusive, shadowy, slippery glimpse of something that drew her as only mathematics had done before.

She came to understand, then, that the art she was to learn to do was in some way indistinguishable from the mathematics of this space. The two impulses were the same at the root. And it was only by following the art down to its origin that she would truly understand the sthanas of Nirx's equations.

In the days between her amnion sessions, Anasuya went in secret to an empty art prep room and practiced making art on the holos there. Manipulating the plotters, she went through the things she had learned in her first years — how to use graphical representations of mathematical functions to create balance and symmetry, resulting in one of the thirty thousand categories of pleasing visual patterns. The textbook exercises served their purpose in helping her re-learn half-forgotten lessons, but they went no further. She tried letting her mind go slack and her hands go wild with the plotter, but the result was ugly and confusing.

Away from the amnion she was hollow-eyed with lack of sleep and filled with frustration. In the amnion she found her happiness in surfing the sthanas, and in each rendezvous with Vara.

But it was becoming too much for her.

One day, sitting in her favorite place in the atrium, she was idly scratching a rash of brown freckles on her forearm, when the Master came up to her.

"Found anything yet, Anasuya?" he lisped eagerly.

She thought of Vara. She thought: yes, I have found a clue, although I don't know where it leads. But she said, only: "Nothing, Master, but what you already know."

"I have some ideas," the Master hissed. "The Nirxian equations must describe some kind of natural system, we know that. But beyond that knowing, we are blind; we grope! You know why, child? Heh! Because as artist-servants of Anhutip we take inspiration from the forms of rocks and sand, but then, we go beyond that to create a poem of our own, our paean to our god. Rarely do we probe the forms of natural things solely to find what mathematical poems they describe. To discover how Anhutip made the world is not the job of the artist. Yet, there are nuances that have not escaped me."

He leaned toward her, a dark shadow topped by the great crimson head.

"I would tell you, but you are so young, so fragile. There are things you don't know, Anasuya, terrible things about the world. I could teach you…"

She shook her head vigorously, slipped to the side along the stone bench and to her feet.

"I must go home," she gasped, and found that she meant it.

She had to get away from him. She took her robe from Amas and half ran out of the Temple doors, down the steps to the plaza. The evening sky was red and purple, and the brightest stars were out. She hadn't been outside the Temple in days. Everything seemed strange. Despite her unpleasant encounter with the

Master she had the sense of being haunted by her visions in the amnion. On the crowded walkways she looked around as though she had never seen the City before. Wherever she looked she saw fragments of the patterns and structure she had seen in the amnion—there, in the architecture of the Temple of the Two Lovers, in the mosaic of its walls; the grains in the faceplates of the woman standing next to her on the walkway; even the sky, with its swathes of color, appeared to be a pale reflection of that strange topography. And when she looked at the faces of the people around her, ordinary people munching the oily, spiced crackers that vendors sold in the evenings, people laughing, arguing, gossiping with each other, sipping nectar from little pipe-straws stuck into gourds—she saw in their brown skin, in the shape of one's forehead, in the set of another's jaw, pieces of Vara…

She shook her head to clear it, and the world seemed to regain some of its normalcy. She remembered Lata telling her: when a quest overwhelms you that can be a good and necessary thing, but not always. When you go swimming in the water, you must remember to come up every so often, to breathe.

What she wanted, needed, was to breathe a little. It was time to go home to her mates.

When Anasuya had first come to the City, it had amazed and bewildered her. Here was legend itself, the place of stone, where the stone people lived. This was what Hasha had seen in his visions. She had wept a little for him, but the place was overwhelming, so fascinating in its austere splendor, its unfamiliar geometries, that old griefs were thrust aside. She lived first near the Temple of the Two Lovers, in the Temple common-house with dry, brown people, their faces half-covered by flat growths of stone, horrified that here were masses of people with no athmis! People blind to her gift, who did not know what the sea was, whose language, over which she had, by now, acquired some mastery—was like sticks and stones being tossed together. In the midst of her confusion there came into her life a thin, pale man whom she had met on the ship that brought her here. His name was Palanik, and he knew some words of her tongue. He was a wanderer, too, like Hasha, but there was nothing restless about him. The City was the place to which he always returned.

Palanik answered her questions, interpreted the customs of the City for her, explained that the moving walkways, the speeders, the light illusions were all made possible by machinery—mathematical art put to use, to make things! She was still unused to the idea, and it shocked her profoundly. There were other things he told her that were incredible: for instance, there were tiny desert polyps, animals that massed together in colonies, building exoskeletons of incredible beauty. On a boulder or a rocky outcrop, he explained, you might see peculiar calcifications: ledges, battlements and ramparts gemmed and veined and studded with minerals that catch the light of the sun and glow deeply in reds and blues, magentas and gold. What the people of the City learned to do was to take this polyp and change it so that it would live in their bodies. With the help of tiny, microscopic machines, these polyps were forced to grow exoskeletons with pre-determined characteristics. Mostly people removed cheekbones or part of the cranium to allow room for these growths, but there were some who had gone in for full-body armor. Anasuya saw these citizens and shuddered. "People of stone," she told Palanik in horrified wonder.

Once, exploring the City, she had wandered off its edge into the desert. "The desert," Palanik had told her, "is the realm of the Nameless Goddess. Her followers are few; they live at the edge of the City or around small oases in the wilderness, and they believe that the desert is both the body and the spirit of the Goddess." Anasuya could hardly believe that people would want to live out in the desert. "How would they get water?" she thought, climbing up a ridge for a better view. The dry, terrible heat, the rocky gullies and dunes so fascinated her that she couldn't turn back even though her body cried out to do so. She wanted to taste the absence of water for the wonder of it. She climbed a dune, staggered down it into a sandy valley and along a rocky gully, wondering at the ridge-like growths of desert polyps — red and green, yellow and purple, like little shelves along the rock wall. It came to her suddenly that the fantastic contortions of rock, the narrow channel that she was walking in had all been shaped by water. Absent now, but leaving its impress with mathematical elegance in the smoothness of the channels, the flaring of hard mineral through soft stone…yes, here there was water, but it was invisible. Then she discovered thirst.

The water bottle she had brought with her was now empty. Climbing back up the valley she found also that she was lost. The sun was high in the sky, her lip had already split once, and she felt faint. In the midst of her fright she had the sense to seek the shade of a rocky outcrop, where, in the deep shadow, she found a patch of damp sand. Some furious digging with her hands revealed a paltry handful of metallic-tasting water, but it was enough for a gulp and for wetting her neck-slits. After that she understood that even in a desert there is water. Eventually, after climbing atop the outcrop and seeing that the City lay to her west, she found her way back. Although she had never returned to this place, she had memorized the path to it that day, standing on the City wall, noting the landmarks. Four years later she could still recall the shock of discovery: the hidden gift of water filtered through rock, gathered from many rains, lying like a moist eyelid in the desert.

When Anasuya had mastered the language and customs of the City, Palanik took her to the Temple of

Mathematical Art. In the beginning it was all joy and frustration: here were people who understood, however imperfectly, what she saw and felt, but they used an awkward language for it and she had to learn it before she could be of any use to them—this harmony was called a Nikoni function, those nested infinities formed a Samke set. Things that seemed obvious to her had to be worked out by them through a series of painful steps they called proofs. She met eager young men and women, anxious to teach her as though she were a very bright child and at the same time in awe of how she saw the world. There had been rumors of such people as herself; she was legend come alive. She met the Master, was duly horrified by him, and luckily found Bakul, who came out of retirement to be her teacher for a brief, difficult, joyful time. Having mastered the strange mathematical language, she learned the rules and techniques for creating mathematical art, obtained a basic grounding in the functioning of the standard vats and chemical mathematics, and mastered the art of mathegraphia.

Ultimately the special amnion was built for her, and she became what she had, in a sense, always been: a rider, an explorer of abstract mathematical countries. The amnion was a relief; before she left her home, she had never been outside water for so long. The spiroforms worked best in water; in air their ability to diffuse was limited, so her mathematical sense was somewhat muted. Her first immersion in the amnion was almost a homecoming.

There were many things that had puzzled her in those early days. Anasuya learned the praise poems to Anhutip and all the lore, but she could not get used to the idea of gods as great, remote, separate beings playing with human lives. "But you Sagarans have gods," Sakanrip, one of the chemists, declared. "Don't you regard the sea as a god and worship those great sea beings?"

He meant the leviathans. But Anasuya didn't know how to explain that the sea, the seaphants and leviathans weren't gods. [If you had the athmis inside you, functional or dormant, how could you separate god from not-god?]

contesting binaries

Which led to another difficult question: what about the people and creatures of the desert, like Sakanrip, who had no athmis? How did they fit into the scheme of things?

Among her own people she had sometimes heard talk of those whose athmis never came to fruition. "What do they do, then? How do they live?" she had asked one of her mothers. "It is a rare affliction, but they live," her mother had said. "It is not that they don't have athmis, just that it does not speak in them. They fish and sleep and love, like anyone. Roru the boat-builder is one such."

Anasuya knew Roru. His boats were swift on the water, but his eyes were always sad.

"They live," her mother had said. "But in a way their lives are not whole. Some of them, I've heard, give themselves back to the leviathans. Your own birthmother had the athmis come to her late, in her thirteenth year. When she was twelve she swam out to the reef to give herself. We stopped her just in time."

Her mother hugged her.

"That's why we were so worried when your athmis didn't blossom until you were five! Yra's athmis gave her the ability to breathe under water and understand the language of the fish. That's why you can stay under water longer than most people! We still don't know why Yra drowned… Oh, had she lived past the first three of your years, she would have been glad of you, Anasuya!"

In her mother's embrace Anasuya had imagined what agonies her birthmother Yra must have gone through. Thank the seas she, Anasuya, had realized her athmis when she did! How terrible to be late, and even worse, to be one of those whose athmis never came into bloom!

Yet it was beyond imagining to be like Amas the doorkeeper. She was sure he had no athmis at all, dormant or not. At first she had found him horrifying, frightening. He was a broken geometry; he contained voids. He was a stone rattling in a gourd. She thought: if I had been born like Amas, I would have wanted my mothers to throw me to the sharks of the deep sea, or, if they didn't think I was too paltry a gift, to take me back to the leviathans. She had never seen his like in Sagara.

Later, Anasuya decided that most of the people of the desert either had athmis that was dormant or had some quality like it that she wasn't able to recognize. Palanik was an exception: she was sure he had athmis, and that it was active in him. She wasn't sure about other people. And yet she could be drawn to them, share laughter, share work, even while conscious of the chasm between them. With Amas, too, she had made progress — her earlier horror had given way to a kind of acceptance. The world is too large for my understanding, she had told herself then, and often since then.

But beneath the challenges, excitement, and novelty of her new life, she had begun to feel hollow. She knew that by leaving the sea she had stepped out of the circle, she was alone — an arc, a segment, a thing broken in both space and time. How do you mend something like that?

"By joining," Palanik had said, kissing her cheek. He took her away from her dry, cell-like dormitory to his own made-house, where she met his mates and at last became part of something: a pentad. The House was a small, irregular white-domed structure at the top of a rocky incline; within were pale arches and pillars of rough stone and rounded walls like the inside of a sphere or a cave. Carved stalactites, delicate as lace, hung from the ceilings; round mica windows looked out like eyes. At its very top was a bubble of a room, a translucent hemisphere that looked up at the sky. A similar bubble let a broad beam of afternoon sunlight into the central common room below. In a small, round room she learned Palanik before all the others, and in her secret mind he was the most beautiful. He wore no gemplates, he was all warm flesh and smooth geometries. He had the clarity, the austere, translucent beauty that she associated with what she would later call linear vector spaces. His studies of social customs took him all over the planet, but there was nothing restless about him; he had a deep, still center, he was home wherever he was.

Her mate Marko worked in the City's food gardens, atop farm towers, planting and tending bottle trees and other shrubs, but he was also a stove-maker and cook. He knew how to capture the sun's light through lenses and make searing platforms and baking ovens — a magician of light and heat! He was quiet, shy, curt, still recovering from the death of his first partner. His outward reserve reminded Anasuya of a difficult algebraic equation: a redefinition of variables, a smile from the heart, and Marko became easy, tractable, his private pain washed out for the moment.

Then there was big Parul, all curves and circular geometries, a spiral shell full of hidden surprises — a topography of all-embracing warmth, even to the amber cheek-plate she wore. Everything about her was effusive and large; she moved with a cloud's grace. She was a technician — she spent days in the hidden world underground with machines large and small that gave the city its coolness and warmth and ease. When Parul came home she liked to eat well, so Marko would cook in a frenzy until the House was filled with aromas of spices and herbs. If all the lovers were present it was especially wonderful; everyone fell in love with everyone else as though the food were an aphrodisiac, and there was an orgy of eating and loving. Then Marko would bring forth his lute, and Palanik would sing in a voice like water and light, and Anasuya would weep for joy, caught in the transient, temporal beauty of the harmonies.

And Lost Silaf would play her melancholy drum. Lost Silaf was the fourth member of the pentad—a small woman, mostly silent, she ministered to them when they were sick. She made love only with Parul; her bond with Marko and Palanik was as innocent and artless as the love between siblings. She had (as yet) no bond with Anasuya that the latter could understand.

Silaf had once been in love with a gwi, one of those winged reptilian creatures that swept across the city skies every winter. Marko told Anasuya the story: Silaf was of a nomadic people called the Ghoomin, and once when her tribe crossed the city during their annual migration, a wounded gwi fell from the sky. She tended him and learned his language and sighed with delight when he told her of the high currents of warm air, the terraces of sky and cloud, the jagged bare peaks of mountains across the desert where he spent the summer. He stayed with her for two seasons even after he recovered. Then one day, when the tribe by chance crossed a migration route, he was roused by the cry of his fellows, and he left her and went spiraling up into the air, calling. But his kind did not know him any more and hacked him to bits before her horrified eyes. When the tribe crossed the city's perimeter again,

Marko found Silaf wandering the streets, crying in the harsh tongue of the gwi, holding a bag of her lover's bones, all polished-white; and he took her in.

Now Lost Silaf spent most of her time in her eyrie, the dome room at the top of the House. Here she tended her garden of herbs and flowers under the well of the sky and knit her lover's bones into abstract sculptures of creatures that did not exist and could not be. Sometimes she sang songs in the tongue of the gwi. To Anasuya Lost Silaf was mainly mystery, a sthanas not completely mapped, a secret geometry whose features were still guessed at. Her face was a delicate sculpting of positive and negative curvatures, her dark, slanting eyes singularities, wells into which Anasuya could imagine falling for ever. Silaf's gaze was disconcertingly frank, as curious and accepting as a child's, which made Anasuya uncomfortable. Anasuya was not yet certain of her feelings for Lost Silaf — she wished she could be as unselfconscious, as comfortable, as unlost as Silaf — both, after all, had come from other places, both had suffered separation from loved ones — yet the space Silaf inhabited was so clear, so much a thing that belonged to Silaf, that Anasuya could only look upon her with a bewildered envy.

Palanik, Marko, Parul, and Silaf. They were her mates. They had given her shelter, respite from loneliness, and love. In her gloomier moments Anasuya felt she had little to give them in return. Her stories, her gift, her athmis were of no value to them. The work she did at the Temple was a thing of wonder and pride to them, but they couldn't understand it, or even what it meant to her. The sea was nothing to them, the leviathans merely wild tales. They were so much at ease in their belonging to each other and to their City that sometimes they inadvertently made her feel the foreigner she was.

What she had to give, she realized, was…gratitude. For saving her from loneliness. For giving her a home in this strange place. What she had to give them was only an echo of their love for her: a wave reflected from a shore.

But all truths, as her mother Lata had once told her, are incomplete.

Anasuya came home after fifteen days away. She stepped off the walkway and climbed up the rise to the House. There were other made-houses nearby, and a cliff-house with windows like eyes, and people clambering up the narrow path before and behind her, talking, laughing. Her neighbors called out greetings to her: "Anasuya! Green Girl! Welcome home!" "How are those star people, those Tiranis, now, we saw it all on the news feeds!" "Stay home a while, Anasuya!" Anasuya, feeling shy and welcomed all at once, waved at them and ran lightly up the steps. Suddenly she remembered that she had forgotten to bring a gift for her mates. All these days away and she had come home with empty hands. She felt shamed by her carelessness, but the white door was already before her. She thought, dismally: when have I ever given them anything? She entered the house feeling small and apologetic.

But inside it smelled like Parul was home, because Marko had a stew bubbling in the big cauldron and the air was full of wonderful aromas. Anasuya was suddenly, ravenously hungry. She entered the common room, and when Palanik and Parul and Marko turned to look at her, she realized from the quality of their silence that they had been waiting for her all this time. They had been talking about her, not laughing or singing before she came in, and Marko had not set out his lute. Moved despite herself, Anasuya held out her arms to them, and the tableau broke into greetings and laughter. But where was Silaf? She looked at Palanik, and he inclined his head up. From above they could hear sounds of strings twanging, like a musician trying to tune an instrument.

Then there were questions, and a plump, brown gourd in her hand, filled with cold windflower nectar. What were the Tiranis like? Why had they traveled through space for a lifetime?

"Eighteen years each way!" Parul said. "So many people they knew and loved will be dead when they go back, won't they, Ana-love? How sad, to be trapped so by time!"

"That's the tragedy of sub-light travel," Palanik said. "There's no way around it, my dears. The laws of reality are thus. The Tiranis must want something very badly to make such a sacrifice. What is it they want, Anasuya?"

Anasuya said: "I don't know. They say it is the mathematics that draws them here. I can see that. It's beautiful, Palanik! A new mathematics, never anything like it before. It's full of mysteries."

She thought about the things she had learned: the dimensionality of the sthanas, with the four-d manifold immersed in it; the fantastic topography being built section by section. Her conviction that it represented some natural system. Those mysterious blank patches, little regions of darkness, ignorance (she had discovered a few more of them in the last few sessions). The Master's obsessive behavior, the way Nirx looked at her as though she wanted to tell her what it was all about, but couldn't. And above all, the mystery of Vara...

But she couldn't explain all this to them. Their responses, however kindly meant, their praise of her amazing mathematical gift, would make her feel awkward, distant, different. Fortunately Marko wanted her to help chop herbs while he added more fuel cakes to the fire. She set about cutting sandhenna and ketelbark into precise little segments, wiping sweat from her forehead and taking a moment to sip her drink. Palanik went to open the little dome in the ceiling and the smoke wafted lazily up.

The cauldron was a great stone bowl, set in the center of a wide depression in the common room. Long rays of light came in through three high windows, converging on the surface of the stew. Marko had arranged the lensing so that the warmth from the sun was just enough to soften and brown the laghori cheese at the top. Parul stirred, her soft laugh ringing out, a gentle ululation, a ripple in the air. Marko added chopped garnishes; Palanik went around pouring wine into the flute glasses. The wine was a dark crimson thread in the glass, refracting the light that fell on it, splashing color on the walls in a wonderful harmony. Anasuya picked up a glass and breathed the red vapor floating above the rim. Already her earlier reservations about her mates were melting away, and love and mathematics were pouring into each of her senses like a flood. All she had to do was to let go, and the answer would come, whatever the question. Palanik dipped the ladle into the stew, blew carefully on to it, and held it to Anasuya's lips. She closed her eyes, tasted it, licked it slowly clean. Palanik watched her smile, his own eyes lighting up. What she wanted to say was that the proportions felt just right, and the flavors felt interestingly biased, in exactly the same way that a nearly symmetric manifold in multiple dimensions made her feel (the stew had at least fifteen ingredients) — but she looked at Palanik through the veil of rising steam and said "it's perfect." Then Palanik was busy dousing the fire, and Marko's lips were against the back of her neck. She turned to embrace him, his warm solidity, the crush of his arms supporting her as she let herself go, become molten in his arms. Palanik offered Parul the ladle; she took a small morsel between pearly teeth and leaned toward him to feed him with her lips. They laughed and kissed, and paused for breath. And right on cue, there was Lost Silaf descending the curved stairway, holding in her arms a harp she had made of her lover's bones, plucking the strings with each step.

Silaf is sitting by the quietly bubbling cauldron, plucking her strange harp. The melody is soft and slow, something they recognize, although it appears to match the tempo of their rising passion: the touch of lip against throat, hand against breast. The ladle is taken around from person to person: food is sacred, its preparation and its feeding is what binds one soul to another. Parul is the one who first begins to feed Lost Silaf; in a few moments she sets the bone harp aside so she can undo the thin gown in which Silaf is clad. Clothes fall to the floor in soft folds, wine flows into throats, over the round of a shoulder, in the hollows between breasts. While the cauldron simmers, the heat in the room rises, there on the low divan, where skin against skin, the lovers couple in all combinations save one. Only Parul is the link to Lost Silaf; Silaf will caress the others but mate only with Parul. Their mutual pleasure is what catalyses the rest of the group. Wine is taken in the mouth and held, and poured in sips from lip to mouth. Anasuya is in a tangle of limbs and breasts, joining, parting to join again; all is soft skin and hard muscle, a lover's breath in her ear, a lover's sigh against her groin. She fits her lower lip against the varying geometries of skin, measuring and tasting curvature, burying her mouth in soft folds, vortex to vortex. All is liquid, like the ocean; the mathematics of one appears to echo that of the other: the circle, the give and take, the forming of something larger than herself, and her own self changing in response. Anasuya senses, in the tangle of lovers' limbs, the aromas of wine and food and passion, something forming, nothing more than a shadow, a memory, of a woman's face in her mind. Vara is a presence, a witness, looking out of the windows of Anasuya's eyes; she is there in the strands of Parul's long, black hair, in the hold of Palanik's long arms, in the flow of Marko's breath on her thigh. She's there only for a moment, that ephemeral creature, but she leaves behind the promise of her return, like the impress of a mouth against a cheek. Anasuya is being swept to sea on a great wave: she is dissolved out of being, into being.

It is in this state of complete receptivity that she is conscious of a seed forming in her mind—the idea ghost that has been haunting her for so many days becoming tangible, although it is no more than a seed. She is careful not to give it much notice. Such a seed only grows when it is not consciously tended. As the lovers dance their slow, ancient dance on the broad divan, the sea ranges over Anasuya: Hasha is in her arms, the wind-trees beat their wild rhythm above their heads. She can sense the relationships, see the congruencies; it is as much the mathematical as the physical (for her there is really no distinction between the two) that makes her cry out in joy and release.

When the joran was over, it was as though they had suddenly fallen back into their bodies from another place. Parul, with low giggles, sat naked on her haunches, mopping up the spilt wine; Palanik straightened the sheets, while Silaf helped Marko ladle stew into large stone bowls. Anasuya, gathering flute glasses, felt sated and bereft all at once. Her own body felt too small to contain her. It was as though (as Palanik had once said) the gods possessed them when they were joined together. As waves of different lengths and frequencies combine together and make something utterly new. She pushed away the feeling of being abandoned and gave herself up to indulging her appetite.

A joran was a rare event because the members of Anasuya's pentad were not always at home at the same time. In traditional pentads, the members traveled together if they traveled at all, and the joran was held on a regular basis, with all due ceremony, with one person, the kendr, as catalyst and initiator. The kendr was the hub around which the wheel turned, and the choosing of the kendr was the first step in establishing the permanency of the pentad. It sometimes took years of living together for it to become clear who the kendr was. Anasuya's pentad was not traditional; there was no kendr, and matings were more often couplings or threesomes, depending on mood and availability as much as anything else. But with or without a kendr, Anasuya felt that the joran made her, for a few moments, almost whole.

She spent two days at home. The night before she left, she had a dream. In the dream she was swimming in the seaweed forests of home when she crossed some kind of invisible boundary and found herself in the vast sthanas of the Nirxian equations. She recognized the silver tangles threading the magnificent geometry, and the dizzying cliffs, valleys, and vortices in between. But how had she gotten from one space to the other? Had there been a door she had passed through? She searched for Vara in the dream, because she was certain Vara had the answers, but instead she found her mother Lata. Lata's silver hair massed about her head like an aureole. "Help me braid my hair," Lata said to Anasuya, but the silver strands were too tangled. "How did you get so far from home?" Lata asked her. Anasuya said: "It was the Trickster wave, mother, it took me, after all." And there was the wave again, sweeping Anasuya away, with Lata receding toward the horizon. Anasuya heard her mother cry out: take this! And Lata loosed a strand of her hair, which became a rope flung out toward her; Anasuya felt it pass between her hands, but her fingers wouldn't close around it.

She woke to the pale light of morning.

She was lying in Palanik's arms. She remembered that she was home, in one of the little round sleep chambers. The circular window was an eye looking out at the world—she saw the mesas gilt-edged with the long rays of the rising sun, the walkways and madehouses already astir with people. She got up carefully, so as to not wake Palanik, and went to the window to breathe in the still-cool air. The air smelled of dust and things to come. Today the amnion would be ready for her again.

Before leaving the House, she kissed Palanik gently, so as not to wake him, and breathed a silent goodbye to the others. She felt her mood lighten, her love for her mates flooding her, making her feel open and tender. She loved them most easily when she was going away.

Red sky, a hundred colors glinting off rock, the landscape in broad swathes of red and gold. Anasuya hopped on a walkway and looked around her. And saw the mathematics of it all, as she used to, but in the new way: the "real" world as bits and pieces, broken shadows, of the sthanas. Or was the real world a strangely refracted version of the vision she had seen, the work of art so profound that she could drown in it and be happy? Vara, come to me today, she said to herself, taking a deep breath of anticipation. The spell was falling on her again. And in her mind the idea seed lay nestled, growing larger, waiting for its moment.

At last there was the Temple mesa on the horizon, red-brown rock thrusting up on the rise like a fortress, and Anhutip's eyes glowing red in the low light of the sun. The absurd thought struck her that Anhutip knew what Nirx's space was all about. Anasuya had always regarded Anhutip as mostly story—how could any of the old desert tales be true, if they left out what was most important to her: the sea? There were no stories about the sea among the desert people. They could not possibly have the whole truth about the universe.

But now she half-believed that Anhutip, trickster and possible pretender, knew just what she was seeking. Help me find it then, old desert lord, she said under her breath, passing underneath his great stone bulk into the cool darkness of the Temple atrium. The door shut behind her, shutting out the world.

The days fell into a routine. Anasuya spent nearly two days at a stretch in the amnion, then two, or sometimes three days outside it, waiting for the molecular mixture to be reconfigured. In that time she made edits and interpolations, which were becoming increasingly complex. Nirx was all admiration.

"Things are so different on Tirana!" Nirx said. "On my world, mathematics is viewed as technology. The study of differential geometry, of dynamical systems, of algebra, all these things we approach with specific applications in mind. So when we want a big picture or a topographical map of something abstract, remote from application, we struggle. This science of mathematical synthesis, of the union of mathematics and art—alas, that science does not exist on my world! We have made little steps on our own, but how much more satisfying to work with the masters! We have not yet learned how to lasso the intuition."

"Is why the Lattice let us go," said the little man Vishk, in his staccato way. He had not completely mastered the language of the City. "Lattice did calculation. Would take long time, hundred years to develop amnion technology, Lattice said. Coming here now more efficient."

He spoke the word "efficient" with reverence. Anasuya had noticed that before.

"Efficiency as a moral principle is not the norm here on Sura," said the Temple chemist Ahran dryly. "Our mathematics came about from half-crazed wanderers in the desert who were visited by the god Anhutip in a dream. When they woke they went to the place he had indicated in the dream, and there they found Anhutip's enormous bones buried in the sand—a great, armored beast he was (you've seen his likeness at the Temple entrance), but broken like a warrior on a battlefield—face plates cracked, cranial plates in five pieces, horned back twisted. So they sang the mathematics to mourn him and revive him. Or so the story goes. In gratitude he set down this Temple, from which his City springs. And he granted to all mathematicians the leisure to live at the City's expense. So all we do here is to make works that praise him. Very inefficient, I'm sure!"

"I envy you greatly," Nirx said. "On my world, everything we wish to do that is outside the norm must be justified. Life is not easy on my world for mathematicians."

"Then stay here," one of the young Temple chemists said, smiling. Her name was Turel, and she glanced at the tall Tirani man, Hiroq, when she spoke. "Stay here with us!"

Nirx shook her head sadly.

"The Conventions of the Lattice of Tirana…"

Anasuya came to recognize this puzzling phrase as a key to change the subject. But she was rarely in the mood for listening to idle chatter. The sthanas she explored in the amnion was so magical and profound, and the work so consuming, that she felt distant from ordinary things.

In the time she had left over from her mathematical explorations, she would slip away to an art prep room, where she had established herself with a holo, and try to create art. Between frustrated attempts she would lie on the couch, sipping tea that Amas brought her, trying to think about what Vara had said, or almost said, at their last rendezvous.

After the first dozen failures at creating art, she decided she was trying too hard. She sat in front of the holo, her hands limply holding the plotters, remembering herself back to the sea. Something simple: waves coming in on a beach. Slowly her hands began to move. By the end she had something.

She started with a parabolic arc, stretched it into sky. Seeded the horizon with mappings that yielded various kinds of fractals when iterated. Littered the gently convex, surface under the sky with sea-flowers and shells whose spirals obeyed the golden ratio. She adjusted color, moved objects around until she had achieved just the right degree of broken symmetry, adjusted the time-dependence of the functions and stepped back. Under the kaleidoscope sky lay a beach where the waves came in with sawtooth regularity, to die on the sand leaving nothing behind but a name.

Spelled out for a barely perceptible moment in the lacy script of sea foam.

Vara.

This is for you, she thought with a fierce, exultant joy.

After that breakthrough things seemed to come easier. She rode the spaces of the amnion with gleeful ease, created art with wild abandon. Although most of what she created had to be quietly deleted at the end, often with tears, she began to understand how to bring something forth from within. Inside her she felt as though things were loosening, shifting. Her internal geometry was morphing in response. She felt the heady exhilaration of being at the verge of something.

In the amnion, at the end of each session, Vara appeared with reassuring regularity. It seemed to Anasuya that the pain and urgency in Vara's eyes was slowly eased with each meeting. Not much was spoken between them, but Anasuya felt that some intangible thing was being transferred to her from Vara each time — and each time she sat before the holo in the art room, that gift would manifest itself in the vistas she created. But she felt, also, that she was giving something back to Vara, easing her pain. She had never given enough to those who had loved her — Lata's death, her own abandonment of the sea and her people, still weighed her down. To be able to give something to someone, even if that person was a ghost in the amnion, assuaged her guilt a little. In return she felt loved, cared for, understood. Because Vara knew her. She was convinced of it. Vara had known her once, perhaps in another body, another form.

It did not take long for the news of Anasuya's artwork to spread. Ahran, the senior chemist, was the first to see it. Before long her old fellow students, some of the senior acolytes, and the Tiranis heard about it and flocked to see it. Her teacher Sozi came waddling in with his gourd and his extravagant gestures and was fulsome with his compliments. She was waving goodbye to him and some others, feeling drunk with praise, when the Master came by.

He looked at each holo carefully, starting and stopping them, then running them again. He ran from holo to holo until the room was filled with dizzying vistas rolling and morphing in time. His mouth widened in a grin of delight. He sucked air through his teeth, making a terrible whistling noise, startling her. When the holos had wound down and the room returned to silence, he said to her:

"At last! You are making gifts almost worthy of Anhutip! I knew it from the day you first came! I will have these displayed in the public halls!"

Before she had time to respond, he put a great, bony finger on her shoulder. She flinched.

"Listen, child, this is what you are meant to do. Not that project for the Tiranis. Forget about that! This is real!"

And he hobbled away.

She realized with a little shock that it had been quite a while since the Master had last questioned her about the meaning of Nirx's equations. In fact she hadn't seen him very much of late. He seemed to have forgotten all about his earlier obsession with the mysterious sthanas.

She shrugged, scratched her shoulder where he had touched her, and went back to gaze at what she had created. She knew, despite the accolades of others, that her pictures were nothing but rungs in a ladder, stepping stones to creating the ultimate work of art. She could see hints and fragments of it in some of her creations, but its time had not yet come. She knew that it would come to her when she understood what Nirx's mathematics was — she was waiting for the confluence of the two mysteries, for enlightenment to come to her at last, but right now she could only imagine it or dream it. She would fall asleep on a couch in the art chamber, dreaming of swimming in the seaweed forest. Vara's face appeared and disappeared in her dream; the leathery green arms of the weeds undulated in the current, spelling Vara's name; the darting of fish outlined her face. To meet and be with someone who understood her so completely after years among strangers, who tapped right into the heart of what it meant to be Anasuya — it was a wild, sweet madness that she didn't want to end.

Her increasing facility with art-making was already beginning to affect her mathematical abilities. She found that when confronted with the little, black, blank spaces that afflicted portions of the sthanas like some kind of sickness, she was better able to guess how to knit the geometry until it was whole. Her instincts had never been so good.

In the last several days she had gotten to know some of the Tiranis better. Nirx was the one she talked to most, by necessity and preference, but she got to know the tall Tirani man, Hiroq, who was in love with Turel, one of the young Temple chemists, and spent as much time with her at the Temple of the Two Lovers as he could. Whenever there was talk of the team returning home across the loneliness of space, Hiroq's face would fall. The others teased him about it, but he was a shy man and would only duck his head and look mournful. Anasuya had already learned to keep her distance from Kzoric, who was rough and bold in her manners and speech, but her hands were delicate and a pleasure to watch when she manipulated the controls on the mixing vats or micro-engineered reaction catalysts. She and Ahran had already had several arguments. The little, bent man, Vishk, was the team calculator, who viewed the world through small, cynical eyes and spoke in disjointed bursts. He lived for numbers—endless matrices of tiny neat numbers in the script of the Tiranis lay spread across his worksheets. There were three others who stayed deferentially in the background, waiting on the others, but Anasuya didn't know them by name.

Anasuya found that she was able to follow the Tirani language now, without much difficulty. It was a flat, sibilant tongue, which had sounded at first like white noise overlaying hints of regularity, but she was now able to follow the patterns, pick out words and (for the most part) map them to meaning and image. She came to realize this when she overheard an impassioned conversation between Nirx and one of the other Tirani women, who served as assistant to Vishk. She understood enough words to reconstruct the conversation.

"…I can never tell him I'm sorry," the woman was saying, her voice full of tears. "Nirx, we'll have been more than thirty-seven years away from home when we return! Oh I wish I'd never come! I wish I were dead!"

"I mourn with you," Nirx said. "My sisters will be dead, and my grandchildren will not know me when I return. But think, Coski, my dear, what it is we are trying to do! If we succeed—oh, how the universe will change!"

Nirx looked up, caught Anasuya's eye. Coski also looked at her. Anasuya could not disguise the fact that she had understood their speech. She was mystified by it, and embarrassed as well. She turned away and busied herself at the holo. After that it seemed to her that the visitors were careful not to hold private conversations in the presence of the Temple folk.

Then the unthinkable happened. Ahran was running a pre-immersion test of the amnion, a check he performed at regular intervals, when he discovered that something was wrong. The holos were registering garbage—random reactions at the edges of giant black spaces. He shouted to the junior chemists to shut off the feed pipes. Anasuya, waiting to step into the amnion, found herself surrounded by a frantic rush of people—holo techs checking settings, the chemists running for test tubes to check the new brew, the micro-techs rolling in their diagnosis machines. She and Nirx stared at each other over the hubbub. What calamity was this?

"It's the chemistry!" Kzoric yelled. The large Tirani woman was in a rage. "Look at this!" she held up a tube of the seed solution, from which the amnion brew had been made. "I checked it only last night—it was clean! Someone has contaminated the seed!"

She looked straight at Ahran. Ahran took a deep breath.

"You are a fool, and a troublemaker" he said. "It is you Tiranis who keep the vat locked. You keep the chemistry of the seed a secret. If the solution is contaminated, it must have been done by one of you!"

Her face working, purple with rage, Kzoric launched herself at Ahran. Two of her colleagues tried to stop her, but she brushed them aside. One of them crashed into the side of the amnion and fell. The other hung on to her again.

Nirx said, in a cold, cutting voice:

"That will be enough from you, Kzoric, or I'll have to remind you why you are here—and where you'll be going."

Kzoric's face darkened. The energy seemed to go out of her suddenly. "As well it could be one of us," she muttered, with an ugly glance at Hiroq. "We all know *he* doesn't want to go home!"

"Nor do you," said Hiroq's lover, Turel, indignantly. But she was silenced by another temple chemist, Vrito. He was shaking with fury.

"Turel, don't go defending those people. Stick to your own kind, if you know what's good."

Vrito spun on his heel and left the room. His footsteps beat an angry retreat in the passageway outside.

Nirx looked at Ahran.

"I presume, Lord Chemist, that you and I can be reasonable about this? Who had access to the locked vats apart from my team?"

"As you know, nobody," Ahran said, speaking with some effort.

"That is not quite true, though," Nirx said gently. "The locking system is used all over your Temple, and anyone with sufficiently advanced skill can probably discover the code. With or without our help. I trust you will take all this into account."

"We can secure the locks, I'm sure," Ahran said stiffly. He unbent a little. "Perhaps it is not sabotage after all, Mathematician. That was Kzoric's notion. Maybe it is just…an error in the reconfiguration process. Perhaps you can re-synthesize the seed."

"That would be difficult, although not impossible," Nirx said. "Fortunately I have kept aside a small supply of the seed for precisely this situation. But tell me, Lord Chemist, what about the amnion?"

"It needs a total chemical cleaning," Ahran said, shaking his head. And then, to Anasuya's dismay, "it will be days before we can use it again."

Distances

It came to Anasuya that while she had been absorbed happily in mathematics and art, there were storms and tensions brewing around her that she had hardly noticed. Kzoric's violence, Vrito's sudden rage at Turel — and even now, the Temple people were standing to one side, the off-worlders to the other, giving each other wary, distrustful glances. Only Turel stood ambiguously in the middle, looking shocked and uncertain.

"This is a serious matter," Nirx said. "Even more if there was danger to Anasuya." She looked questioningly at Ahran.

"There might have been," Ahran said, frowning worriedly. "We have to finish analyzing the contaminants. It is a good thing you weren't in there, Anasuya!"

"Yes, indeed a good thing," Nirx said, taking Anasuya by the arm and leading her out of the room. As they left, Kzoric directed a look of hatred at Anasuya. "Yes, we can't afford to lose the green fish," she muttered under her breath. Nirx appeared not to have heard.

Later, Anasuya asked Ahran what Nirx had meant by the remark about Kzoric. Why had Kzoric to be reminded why she was here — and where was she going? It turned out that Kzoric had an ugly past on Tirana. She had killed two people in a violent rage and had had to be confined permanently away from society. But thanks to Tirani law she could exchange part of her solitary confinement for a service that involved risk and danger. She had been a chemist, so she offered her services for the long trip through space with

Nirx's team. Unfortunately she had assumed that the time dilation would commute her sentence, but Nirx had recently informed her that the law had provisions for such things. When Kzoric went back, it would be to go into solitary confinement again, unless she found another, similar project to volunteer with.

Of course Ahran knew this because Turel had told him, and Turel had learned it from her lover Hiroq.

"But I think it is not impossible it was Hiroq himself who poisoned the brew," Ahran told Anasuya. "He looks quiet and shy, but he's crazy about Turel, and she's not going back to his world with him. And the Tiranis aren't going to let him stay on either — their Lattice is quite strict about that."

He smiled at Anasuya. "Don't worry about these things," he said. "You have your mathematics — leave the handling of people to Nirx and me!"

So Anasuya did. She worked at her art, although she missed Vara and the sthanas of Nirx's equations. Meanwhile Nirx and Ahran seemed to be making a concerted effort to bring the two distrustful teams together. There were group feastings, an outing to a couple of Temple events. The amnion was being scrubbed and the chemicals were almost ready. Things were going to return to normal, even though the alleged saboteur had not been discovered. The two teams began to relax a little, although Kzoric was sulky and distant, and most others, including members of her own team, remained wary of her.

Distances

The Temple organized a trip to the oasis of Vehda, which was a site of pilgrimage for followers of the Nameless Goddess. It was a hot, dry, breathless trip in a long speeder that swished over the sand, raising dust plumes as they went. Here the visitors admired the great water-trees, with their enormous, swollen trunks, and the small pool under the overhang of black cliffs. The caves in the cliff were occupied by the Goddess's devotees, white-cowled and reticent. Ahran tried to explain to the guests something of their philosophy.

"The Nameless Goddess is an old rival of Anhutip, but she's older than he is. Her people claim that not only is she the only real thing in the universe, she is greater than reality. She is what holds reality, they say, whatever that means. They say that her followers always find water, even if they are dying in the desert. Or rather, water finds them, if they are far away from the oasis. They say the desert is riddled with hidden paths that the water takes, you know, little short-cuts through a greater reality."

Nirx was interested in this view of reality.

"So, there is a meta-reality, you say?"

"*I* don't say," Ahran said, good-humoredly. "But yes, you could call it that. Her followers believe that the world is an illusion. The Nameless Goddess is a great illusionist, so I can see that. You know — one moment, calm sand dunes, another moment, a sand-storm. And mirages. So the paths and connections in this world aren't the only ones. Because this world is embedded in the greater reality. Which is the Nameless Goddess."

"They've produced one great mathematician," said another chemist. Her name was Panjar and she was Ahran's contemporary. "You remember, Ahran, that odd man? He used to come and use our archives, when we were junior acolytes. Kar-Pthath, his name was. He was always talking about pathways through meta-reality. Wanted to discover how our reality lay coiled in the body of the Goddess. Half-roasted he was, with all his days in the sun—dark as night, crazy as a whittling-bug, but his mathematics was sound."

Nirx announced that she wanted to hear more old tales.

"Then we should take you to a telling," Turel said, delighted. "Hiroq has already gone to one. At the Temple of the Two Lovers. They tell the best stories."

The Tale of the Two Lovers: A Telling

When Time was young, Ekatip and Shunyatip were always together. They loved and they played, and they wandered far and wide through the seas of sand, because at that time there really wasn't much else in the world. They took the forms of men and women according to their whim, and found all the different ways to join together in love. During their wanderings they discovered the secret of Number, which they kept hidden in a cube made of bone. This magic cube gave them the power to count, to draw maps and to make sense of the world.

One day a desert wind came up and wrapped a rope of sand around Shunyatip. Shunyatip yelled for help, and Ekatip took hold of him so that the Nameless Goddess could not have him. But she was strong — so strong that the two of them started being pulled away toward a dark cave that opened in a cliff not far from them. In desperation Shunyatip invoked the god of air and fire, who came in a female form and tried to help them. But it was of no avail, for the three of them found themselves pulled into the cavern and flung to the floor. The noose of sand then loosened and became a beautiful woman who enticed them to mate with her. Dazzled by her beauty, the two Lovers and the god of air and fire cavorted in a fine orgy with the woman, who was none but the Nameless Goddess herself. But Shunyatip, who had the magic cube, was suspicious, so he hid it in his mouth just before the Goddess undressed him. When she put her tongue in his mouth, it felt so much like hot sand that he nearly swallowed the cube, but she didn't find it, even though she searched his body, and that of Ekatip, with her groping sandy fingers. The mating was so passionate and frenzied that nobody noticed when a fifth person joined the group. Or if they did, they didn't care. When it was all over they found that the stranger was the lesser god Anhutip himself, who was known as a mischief maker. He was not very powerful, his only talent being to change the appearance of things, including himself, so that he could do the sneaky things for which he was known. So, for instance, instead of his usual lizard-like form, he had taken the form of a handsome young man, but of course, nobody was fooled. As they put their clothes on, somewhat embarrassed, they turned to find that the Nameless goddess had vanished, and there was only a heap of sand on the floor of the cave. The sand raised itself up into a whirlwind and whirled them out of the cave, where they found a proper sandstorm brewing, always a sign of the Nameless Goddess's anger or disappointment. The god of air and fire said her goodbyes and vanished; Anhutip changed back into his lizard-like form and burrowed furiously into the sand until there was no sign of him at all.

Shunyatip made sure that he could still feel the cube in his mouth, and he and Ekatip set off to find shelter until the goddess's anger had passed. They found a small, rocky cave where they crouched together, waiting. But when Shunyatip took the cube out of his mouth he found that what he held in his hand was a stone. The magic cube was gone. He flung the stone away in disgust, shook out his clothes, but no cube. Immediately the two lovers realized that Anhutip must have stolen the cube in the middle of the orgy and exchanged it with the stone. The god of air and fire couldn't have done it because she was their ally, and besides, they could see into her mind, which was as clear as clear mica. So they decided that they needed to peer into the past to see at what point Anhutip had stolen the cube, and into the future to see where he

Distances

might have hidden it. Whichever of us finds it first, Ekatip said, must jump in time to where the other one is and let him know.

By now the storm was over, so they crept out of the cave and looked around them. There was nothing but sand and rock and sky. So they sat down, back to back, and began to peer into time, step by step. They did not notice when Anhutip, in the form of a small desert lizard, crept close to them and retrieved the stone that Shunyatip had spat out of his mouth. Because all he had done was to change the appearance of the cube to look like a stone. As soon as he touched it, it turned into a cube again, and off he went with it.

Now that the two lovers had the cube no longer, they had no more mastery over Number. So they lost count of how many steps back and forward in time they had gone. Realizing this, they stopped counting. Now each waits for the other to jump up to him in time, so that they will be together again.

In all the eons that have passed they have forgotten about the cube and seek only each other. Each hopes that the other will jump ahead or backward in time to meet him. Each wonders whether they should keep walking in time in opposite directions so that they will meet at last. They do not realize that all they have to do to break the spell is turn around and see each other.

As for Anhutip, he took the magic cube and learned more from it than the Two Lovers ever had. When he had learned it all he swallowed it and kept it in his body until he had understood all forms and relations. After he had done so, he breathed out the world as it is now, in all its diverse splendor. Instead of just sand and rock and empty sky, there was, for the first time, water. And stars. And all the creatures of the world, like us.

Of course there are those who worship the Nameless Goddess who claim that she was the one who got the cube. According to them, she sent up that sandstorm to throw suspicion away from herself. In truth, they say, when Anhutip heard the rumors spread by the followers of Ekatip and Shunyatip that he was the one who had stolen the cube, he was too proud to deny them. Being a sneaky, deceptive sort of fellow, he set himself up as the Mathematician who brought the world into being, when it was really the Nameless Goddess. They call him Anhutip the Pretender.

When we ask them why the Nameless Goddess doesn't come out and tell everyone the truth (if it is the truth, which we doubt) her followers point to her contrary nature and her love of solitude. She does not want the veneration of the masses or cities built in her honor. She hates settlements, civilization, order. All she desires are her few devotees, the loneliness of the desert, and the sigh of the sand dunes in the wind.

Idea ghosts are insubstantial things. When they form seeds they become a little more tangible; they must be tended carefully, fed the right stimuli, without being over-watered or too frequently examined. They must be allowed to grow in the dark of the mind.

And so it was, with Anasuya.

She had been aware for a long time that it was important to know what natural system Nirx's mathematics represented. Not because the Master had once urged her to find out, but because it was the key to her own understanding of the sthanas and possibly to Vara's identity as well. Nirx and her group had maintained that the mathematics described no known natural system; that it was something invented or discovered by Nirx while she was studying abstract representations of the entity called the Lattice on Tirana. The Lattice connected every human on Tirana to every other human; it was physical but had grown organically, a mesh of connections and hierarchies, social relations, governing bodies and knowledge structures with both history and geography. Nirx's team maintained that the Lattice was the inspiration behind Nirx's discovery of the new sthanas, although the Lattice was only the launching point, the idea seed that had given rise to Nirx's equations.

But Anasuya had realized very quickly that whether or not the Lattice had been Nirx's starting point, the sthanas where the equations lived was too complex and beautiful to represent anything but a natural system. The Master had known that as well, although he seemed no longer interested in the answer. What Anasuya had to do was to study the sthanas as well as she could and wait for the answer to form in her mind.

The day came when the idea seed became more than a seed.

That day she was standing in nervous anticipation before a holocube in the art prep room, about to make the first brush-strokes of her masterpiece.

She was approaching the whole thing in a careful, yet oblique way, letting her hands move the plotters as though she were a boat in a wild sea. What she had to do to capture the beauty of the vision she had had so long ago in the amnion—the vision of the greatest work of mathematical art in the universe that was not the universe itself—was to create it around Vara. Vara as mathematics, as the sea, and Vara the woman, clothed in mystery. She felt that if she could create this work of art, she would be able to answer who or what was Vara.

Working at the holo with a sort of studied casualness, as though she were not doing anything of much importance, she found herself sketching in little details of the sthanas of Nirx's equations. Valleys, contours, tessellations. Vara's hair coiling, silver lines threading the space.

She didn't dare do too much. This was just a sketch.

When she let go of the plotters, she felt it: the idea seed becoming as weighty as an egg. She was unable to do any more work; she felt prickly with impatience, restless to return again to the amnion.

"Heh!" the Master said, in his usual sudden way, making her jump. He was at the door of her room, a looming darkness topped with crimson light. He didn't look at her but went straight to the holo. He peered at it, went around it, clucking and nodding to himself, rubbing his teeth-bristles together in the way that made Anasuya wince. She stood silently as far away from him as possible, wishing he would go away, but also curious. Why was he here, bothering her after so many days of leaving her alone?

"You are working with that sthanas the Tiranis brought, still?" he barked, looking at her for the first time. Anasuya nodded.

"Very difficult, still, isn't it? Wasting all those hours on that nonsense, dancing to the foreigners' whims! Haven't found out what that sthanas means, have you?"

He gave her an unexpectedly sly look. Anasuya shook her head, startled.

"Heh! You have something happening in this holo," he said, jabbing in its direction. "Very suggestive. Some real art, maybe, if you work at it. I want you to stop wasting time and finish this!"

He turned on his heel and was gone. She heard his footsteps, quick, irregular, in the stone corridor. He had disturbed her in a way she didn't completely understand. Perhaps he was really going mad. There had been rumors.

During the next couple of days she avoided working at the holo with the rough sketches and tinkered with some of the other, more complete art projects: adjusting the time flow here, making a change in the geometry morphing matrix there. Every once in a while she would look at the new, incomplete holo and wonder what the Master had seen in its unfinished, barely hinted-at landscapes. The idea seed that was now as round and heavy as an egg lay quiescent in her mind. She was terrified it would melt away. She felt jumpy and annoyed with everything, and knew it was simply an agony of waiting. Waiting for the amnion to be ready...

When the amnion was ready, she went to it the way a desert wanderer returns to an oasis. She saw in her mind's eye—the confluence of the mathematics and art, the place to which she had to swim. It was there, just a few stroke-lengths away. At last.

She had not realized to what extent the sthanas had become home to her until she was immersed in it again. The first few minutes she spent flying through it in sheer delight, revisiting familiar features and territories. Then she got to work, mapping and charting as usual—and waiting.

Some instinct nudged her to follow along one of the silver lines, which, she knew, were curves where the four-d subspace intersected itself. She imagined what it would be like to be confined to that four-d space, unaware of the fact that it was immersed in the seven-d sthanas. A memory came to her from her childhood: watching a water beetle crawl along a long seaweed frond that lay folded and tattered, washed up on the beach after a storm. The small creature had followed the undulations of the frond until it reached the nutrient-filled node on the tip, which was folded almost directly beneath the beetle's starting point. "All you had

Distances

to do," she told the beetle, "was to let yourself drop down from where you started!"

She remembered the dream that had come to her not long ago. Lata being swept away from her, toward the horizon, flinging toward her the life-line, a silver strand of her hair. She recalled how, when Vara's image broke up after each meeting, her hair would come adrift from her head, the strands floating away. She had been trying to capture that in her latest work of art. And suddenly there was an explosion in her head: she thought of the great void that separated both her and Nirx from their homes, she thought about what the Master had exclaimed to her long ago, she thought of an overheard conversation between Nirx and one of the other Tiranis, and she remembered the mathematician who had been a follower of the Nameless Goddess: Kar-Pthath, who had wanted to discover how our reality lay coiled within the body of the Goddess. And it came to her why the Tiranis would travel for eighteen years each way for this secret.

Somehow she kept the knowledge inside her through the long session in the amnion. When it came time to meet Vara, she realized that Vara had been hinting something to her all along; she simply had not been able to read Vara's lips until now.

I have no time, Vara had been saying, offering Anasuya the gift of art. Take an empty space and create something in it.

Space and time…

Anasuya didn't breathe a word of this when she finally emerged from the amnion. She scrubbed perfunctorily in the shower, impatiently let the chemists examine her for signs of toxicity, and forced herself to sit at the holo afterward and do corrections and interpolations across the little dark patches of blank space. Ignoring Nirx's curious glance, she left the room as soon as she could and went straight to the Temple archives. She had been two days in the amnion, and she was faint with the effort and with the shock of discovery. But this could not wait.

She asked the senior archivist for anything he might have on Kar-Pthath. She learned that Kar-Pthath had died only a few years before she had come to the Temple. Scrolling through holos about him and his mathematics, she discovered interesting echoes of the Nirxian equations, although where Nirx's mathematics was complex and explicit, what Kar-Pthath had come up with was shadowy and vague. But suggestive. He, too, had come up with a four-d manifold with the same $(1,1,1,-1)$ metric. There was more than an analogical connection.

Trembling with the weight of her new knowledge, she walked into the analysis room. It was busy as usual—the Tiranis were rolling the vats into the storage rooms, Nirx was going through the holos and speaking in a low tone to her calculator, Vishk, while Ahran, along with a small knot of other chemists, was checking the integrity of the micro-machines.

She stood in the entrance until Ahran saw her face and stopped what he was doing. The room followed suit.

"What is it?" Nirx asked, with a faint note of anxiety in her voice.

"I have found out the secret," Anasuya said, in a too-loud voice that trembled. "This sthanas of Nirx's equations. It is the geometry of meta-reality. The four-d manifold is our space and time. The silver lines, the self-intersections of the four-d manifold, mean that there are short-cuts through the topography of the sthanas! That is why you came here, did you not? To find out how to navigate meta-reality? Why did you not tell us?"

There was dead silence in the room, only the low hum of the diagnostic machines. The Tiranis looked at each other. There was suppressed emotion on Nirx's face, which Anasuya couldn't read.

At last Ahran spoke.

"Mathematician Nirx, is this true?"

Nirx bowed her head. It was as much admission as apology.

"I wondered…when you'd find out. Only, we don't call it meta-reality. Perhaps it is not so large a thing. We call it by many names: hyperspace, the greater beyond. It is a physical space that undergirds our own, in which our space is immersed. A lone spacer discovered it by chance and paid for it with her life, but it was not in vain. We got enough information from her craft's machines to reconstruct some of the mathematics of this higher-dimensional space."

She was smiling, now. She stood straighter, as though a burden had fallen from her shoulders.

"Before we left Tirana," Nirx continued, "the Lattice instructed us to withhold this information from you. I was against that from the start. Here we were, about to find a way to free humanity from the tyranny of sub-light travel—to bring people together at last—and they wanted us to keep this a secret! I am relieved that it is out now, thanks to you, Anasuya."

"So if Anasuya hadn't found out," Ahran said, coldly, "you would have returned to your planet with this secret. Having used us, used our mathematics and our labor to discover the truth, you would have simply gone away with the prize. You talk of freeing humanity, bringing people together, Mathematician. Yet you kept all this a secret—you had your seed solution locked up, kept its formula from us so we could not reproduce it!"

"My Lord Chemist," Nirx said unhappily, "much of what you say is true. Yet consider. Did Anasuya make this discovery entirely on her own? Have I not dropped hints? Was it not I who asked to go to the Vehda oasis, knowing in advance about the legends of the Nameless Goddess and the curious parallels between my mathematics and her philosophies? I would not have left—" and here she looked defiantly at her shocked, silent team before returning her gaze to Ahran—"I would not have left without making sure that you knew!"

A tense silence fell.

At last, Ahran sighed and squared his shoulders.

"The amnion is no longer available for study until we have discussed this. Not just the Temple directorate but the City council should debate the continuance of this project."

"Debate it, as is your right," said Nirx, quelling heated protests from her team. "But place before the Temple and the City my offer. From now on, we are willing to share all information. Remember, Lord Chemist, that it takes us eighteen of your years to return to Tirana, and fourteen years for the messages, with our calculations, to reach our world at light-speed. You have fourteen years of lead time to develop your own ideas, your own technology. In that time perhaps you can build the first ship that leaps across hundreds of light-years in almost no time! My world offers your City a treaty of peace and cooperation that was written with just this circumstance in mind. Together we can help make humanity one family again."

Through the excited buzz of exclamations, protests, and argument, only Anasuya stood silent, bewildered. Thinking: what have I let loose here? For a moment she thought of Hasha's visions, people in little steel capsules traveling across space like seeds in a pod. Only, now there was the chance that they could leave one day and be back the next day, or the next. Nirx and her team had lost some of their loved ones for ever; in the future, lovers would no longer be sundered by time or space.

But they should have shared all this. The secrecy, the dishonesty, was like a bad taste in the mouth. Nirx was looking at her across the room, her eyes sad, apologetic. It was true, Nirx had tried to drop hints. Anasuya didn't know if she would have arrived at the truth without them. Maybe not so quickly. It was as much Lata and Vara and the sea that had guided her to the answer. And her mates, through the joran, which had brought forth the idea seed. And even the Master, and the two Lovers, and the Nameless Goddess had been her guides.

But now it was all over, at least for a while. What was left while the high councils debated? What was left for Anasuya to do?

She left the room and made her way to the atrium. Here, in the dappled light, it was peaceful. The bristle-worms swam in the near-dark of the pool, blinking softly at each other. Anasuya scratched vaguely at the freckles on her arm, allowing her thoughts to drift. She was still shaken by the deceit practiced by the Tiranis, Nirx's efforts notwithstanding. But she didn't want to think about that, or about the implications of near-instantaneous travel. What she wanted was to get back into the amnion and explore this space with her new knowledge. If the four-d manifold was spacetime, then what did the remaining three dimensions mean? How did the sthanas as a whole relate to our reality?

She thought of Vara. She, Anasuya, had solved the mystery of what the sthanas represented, and she had thought that would tell her who Vara was. But Vara was still a mystery. Who was she? Where had she known Anasuya, and when? That question remained unanswered.

And what had Vara meant by "I have no time?" If the project continued, then one day it would end, and

Distances

the Tiranis would go home. And there would be no Vara, unless there were more amnion sessions, unless the peace and cooperation treaty were signed and the secret of the seed solution shared. Anasuya didn't want to think about a life without Vara.

Suddenly Anasuya felt panicked, as though all the time left in the world were running out this very moment. She had to get back in the amnion. She had to see Vara again and be reassured that Vara would still be there. That Vara wasn't going away, ever.

But that was impossible.

She went to the art prep room that had been given her for her exclusive use. She looked at the rough outline she had made, of her greatest work of art. Looking at it, she felt it was a small, poorly done thing that would come to nothing. Vara wasn't in it. Vara...

Viciously, she jabbed the wipe button. The shapes and colors bled away, leaving behind a featureless white terrain.

She sank down on the floor and wept.

In those tense days, the City debated, the Temple directorate met day after day. Nirx was often in the meetings, emerging exhausted, looking her age. But the conclusion was foregone. A discovery of this magnitude, leading to technologies that nobody had dreamed of before — the City could not let that go. The project would be completed.

But the project was not without detractors. The Master came to Anasuya, begging her not to continue. "Art!" he said in his mad way, glaring at her, smiling his ferocious smile. "That is what you have to do, Anasuya. Don't complete the Tirani project! Finish what you started that night, in the art room." And Turel came to her in tears and would not say what she wanted, although it was clear. Turel wanted Hiroq, and they wanted each other so badly that perhaps they no longer cared so much about the project. Even Kzoric found her one afternoon, when Anasuya was standing before the Temple doors, at the top of the great flight of stairs, looking over the city-scape. Kzoric came up so silently that by the time Anasuya felt her presence, Kzoric had already gotten a hand on Anasuya's waist. Anasuya staggered, almost losing her balance, but Kzoric caught her to her.

"Can't have you falling about," she said breathlessly. "Little green girl, how about spending some time?"

Anasuya wriggled out of her grasp. Then suddenly Amas was there, with his broad, puzzled face filled with concern. "Do you want some tea?" he asked Anasuya, glancing timidly at Kzoric. Kzoric cursed under her breath, looked at Anasuya.

"Listen, I want you to go slow, you know! Take time. Don't hurry. Come to me, I'll make it worth your while."

Distances

She walked heavily into the atrium, where her footsteps echoed for a long time.

Anasuya smiled at Amas, taking the tea from him although she felt too sick to drink it. Her hand trembled, spilling some of the tea. What had Kzoric meant? How dare she threaten Anasuya, the Temple's best rider? She determined to tell Nirx and Ahran about the encounter at once. Thank goodness for Amas!

She squeezed his shoulder. "You are wonderful," she told him, leaving him to a perplexed joy.

The debate was all over the newsfeeds. Anasuya's own image was there too, but she hated watching herself on the news feeds because it reminded her of how foreign she was. Going home on the walkways and tube-cars, she would be besieged by questions from the citizenry, to which she could only reply: wait and see. The City that had taken her in, as it took in everything and everyone in its indiscriminate way, absorbing them all into its matrix, suddenly rediscovered her. She was interviewed, followed, imitated—people began to color themselves in stripes and patterns of green unguent (green was apparently the new red), and her art became the rage. The Temple had never had so many visitors come to its public halls, or so many credits roll into its already vast accounts. The citizenry walked around the holos, exclaiming, while the acolytes expounded and sold mathematical trinkets. It was all for the greater glory of Anhutip. Anasuya's mates came, all but Silaf, who rarely left home, and were duly awed and proud. She was pleased and embarrassed, but most of all she longed for the peace and anonymity of her earlier existence. The routines of the day, the pleasures of the amnion, the gift of Vara's presence. Going home became difficult—she did not want to answer any more questions on the walkways or speeders. Outside her home, too, there was little peace, because the news people came with their nosiness and spyers, their busy mechanical recorders and curious eyes. So she began to keep to the quiet places in the Temple.

At last the verdict was out. The Temple directorate and the City Council both concluded that the project would continue and that after this point there would be no more secrecy between the teams. The great map of hyperspace, that most elegant and complex of sthanas, would be completed. After all, one couldn't make half an offering to Anhutip. Messages were sent from the spaceport in Tilfax, the City's equatorial outpost, to let the Tirani government know that their proposal of peaceful cooperation had been accepted. Spaceport engineers were called to the Temple so that they could be informed about developments. Their mandate would be to apply the knowledge of this hyperspace to build a ship. The engineers on board the Tirani ship would help them. Anhutip's mathematics would enable his people to navigate the universe!

"The age of the slow-ships will soon be over," the City Council proclaimed, after it announced the decision. The Temple directorate had unanimously come to the same decision, with one abstention. The Master had not been at the meeting.

For Anasuya, the verdict meant a return to the rhythms of her earlier life. She had made some progress with her art, but she needed Vara to infuse her with the fire it took to completely conceptualize it. And the new sthanas — hyperspace — called to her as much as it had done before.

Except that this time there was a focus to her work, where earlier it had been much more of a free exploration. "Now I can tell you what I really want you to do," Nirx told her, smiling. "You've already discovered the significance of the silver lines, the intersection curves. What we must do now is to look along the intersection lines for the places where we can make hyperspatial jumps. These will occur where the tensor fields of the sthanas interact with ordinary matter fields. You see?"

In her mind's eye, Anasuya saw it: space and time dimpled and twisted by burning suns, or massive black holes, interacting with the tensor fields of the higher-dimensional sthanas. In the dynamically complex, tortured regions around extreme concentrations of matter, there were smaller eddies in spacetime, second order effects that created openings into the higher-dimensional space, and back. Hyperspatial jump points! These special spots were given away by certain peculiarities of the local curvature and torsion. She knew these places; she had seen them. But how to recognize, in the greater universe of the sthanas, the familiar landmarks of her own spacetime neighborhood? How to unfold the four-d manifold and make a one-to-one correspondence between points on it and points on a ship's star chart? As though anticipating the question, Nirx said:

"Of course, ultimately we must make a mapping from the sthanas to our space. To do this we need a familiar starting point. I've calculated one — with the help of Vishk — from your earlier data. That's all we've been doing, all these days the project was at a standstill. We can pinpoint the neighborhood of the Tirana star system in the sthanas…"

"How did you do that?" Anasuya asked, amazed.

Nirx said: "It was…very difficult. I will tell you about it some time. It has to do with the fact that Tirana orbits a binary star system with some very peculiar features. But given this one element of the mapping, can you find the rest?"

Anasuya dutifully began this task, but she felt constrained by it. To her it seemed as though the focus on the four-d manifold, although understandable, was missing something important. It was in the higher dimensional sthanas as a whole that the most interesting mathematics was buried. The deepest secrets were there: the true relation between space and time, between four-d and the other dimensions, between matter fields and the exotic denizens of the sthanas. Here past and future were tangled like lovers' limbs. But there was no time to explore this.

She told Nirx this, once. They were both sitting in the refectory, sipping tea. Light came in through the lattice of mica windows, dappling the floor with yellow parallelograms. Anasuya was shy about telling Nirx how she felt. She scratched a freckle on her thigh, examined the webbing between her fingers, and after a couple of false starts, gave voice to her dissatisfaction.

"If we study only our own spacetime," Anasuya said, a little stiffly, "our knowledge of hyperspace remains incomplete. I believe, Mathematician, that the four-d manifold emerges from the way space and time and various matter fields interact in the sthanas. That is what we must study!"

Nirx said:

"I sympathize with you, Anasuya, because I, too, am a mathematician before anything else. But this practical problem we have set ourselves is also of great importance. To think that in some future age my people and yours will be able to travel without saying goodbye forever to their loved ones—when we will be able to share our separate wisdoms—that is a great thing, Anasuya!"

Of course, that is a great thing, Anasuya thought. But this focus on the four-d manifold and star charts leaves out so much... She said nothing.

"I've always sensed humanity's loneliness," Nirx said. "I...I had someone once, a man I loved, who went away. He used to fly experimental spaceships, research ships that tested new technologies. He went away on an experimental mission, trying to go further than anyone had ever gone before. He never came back."

"Oh," Anasuya said. She didn't know what else to say. Her mind went, for an instant, to Hasha. Who could have known that the kindly, self-possessed Nirx had suffered like that as well!

Nirx's gaze was distant, brooding. After a while she blinked, and smiled apologetically at Anasuya.

"Never mind all that," she said. "It happened a long time ago. Tell me more about how you think, Anasuya. I've seen in your mind a place where mathematics remains pure, untainted by thought of application or use. Tell me, have you never thought about the uses of things?"

Anasuya shook her head slowly.

"I was discouraged from thinking about the uses of things," she said. She didn't want to say any more. She remembered once, early in her time with Lata, she had become impatient with the learning of the harmonies of ripples in still water. She was getting it all wrong, and in frustration the child Anasuya had said: what is it for? What she meant was: I can see it, why do I have to learn the names, to say it? But Lata, taking her words another way, had spat out the saltweed she had been chewing and said to her with great seriousness: the orders and patterns of the world are meant to be discovered, experienced, and celebrated. To ask what they are for is a meaningless question, because they simply are. To use them, to apply them, is to step outside the world, to no longer experience it. Only some knowledge can be utilized for our needs, and that too with great circumspection…

The young Anasuya had nodded solemnly then, not knowing that she would one day betray all that. Then there had been an innocence in the world, or in her knowledge of it. Lata had told her to keep her mind as open as a curved palm: curved so that the water in it wouldn't run out, and open so she could truly see the world.

She looked at her hands. She was afraid that if she spoke, Lata would speak through her, condemn her, Anasuya, out of her own mouth, call her a betrayer because she had taken the most subtle and beautiful harmonies of the world and let others put them to mundane use, however noble the motives. And if Lata spoke, Anasuya would have to stop what she was doing. Hyperspace, with all its astonishing beauty and mystery, and Vara, whose eyes burned with a message for Anasuya alone—all that would be lost to her. If that happened she would die, she knew that. So she kept silent.

Nirx said, gently into the silence:

"One of the most wonderful things about your planet is that there is so much difference, from one place to another. So many cultures and peoples, each with their own stories. Do you know, my planet, Tirana, is like one city? The entire planet, I mean. There are many cities, and towns, and villages, but they all feel and look the same, except for size. On Tirana it does not matter so much where you live, because our technology connects us to each other. We don't even have anything like the Temple directorate. Instead we have the Lattice, which…oh, it is hard to explain! It is what connects us to each other, but it is also an entity that governs. It keeps the peace, rounds out the edges, recycles our stories. So everyone, for the most part, wants the same things and lives the same way. We don't have many adventurers, but we cherish the few we have. Like my team."

Anasuya couldn't imagine it. All those people — millions of them, from what she had heard. With their athmis absent or dormant, living connected lives that were copies of each other? It made no sense.

"Are you saying people never get lonely in your world?" she asked.

Nirx shook her head.

"There are all kinds of loneliness. Many people on my world don't even know they are lonely. The Lattice is their reality, their sickness and comfort. And yet… Haven't you ever felt lonely in a crowd?"

This was such a familiar feeling for Anasuya that for a moment she couldn't speak. Traveling on the City walkways or speeders. Waking up in the arms of her lovers. She nodded. Yes, she knew how that felt.

Nirx said:

"Tell me a little of your people. I've heard the stories of Anhutip, and the Two Lovers, and something of the Nameless Goddess, but not much about Sagara."

Sagara. The sound of the name was enough to bring pain. How to tell someone who hadn't been there about an entire universe? Since they had been talking about loneliness and lovers, the first thing Anasuya thought of was Hasha. And the one time she had been alone during her childhood. She didn't want to tell Nirx about that, because the memory was painful. It had to do with the story of the Cave of Delusion—she couldn't tell Nirx the personal part of the story, she thought. But she remembered.

When Anasuya was growing up, she had heard many times the story of the Cave of Delusion, but it had never occurred to her to go looking for it. It occurred to Hasha, however, and he got some of the young people so excited about it that they went exploring every crack and crevice in the cliff-face at the north edge of the bay. The large caves were used for shelter during the Season of the Rains, but there were plenty of smaller ones. None of them led to the place they were seeking, however.

At last Hasha had an idea that startled them even more. He wanted to look for the cave in the place of the ancestors! This was a place where the sea had flung an arm over the land: a long, narrow, twisting fjord, a backwater connected to the ocean through a labyrinth of passageways, most of which remained under water permanently. It was impossible to climb down to the fjord from land, so it was only approachable from the sea at low tide, when some of the passageways became clear of water. Along the rock walls of the fjord were inscribed, in an ancient script, the saga of the children of the sea. It was a sacred place. Here were clan-poems rendered in a complex script, learned and practiced only by a few. Here were works of art: circles and spirals entwined, fish and people, seaphants delivering benediction, each drawing revealing layers and layers of meaning. The sea's own script was written here, in the shape of the rock wall and what was covered at high tide and revealed at low. The greatest songs ever written were recorded here, including mathematical poems in a script more sophisticated than the ordinary one, the script Anasuya would begin to learn, slowly and painfully, in her last year with Lata.

To go into the place of the ancestors with any purpose beyond that of creating or contemplating was unheard of. Some of the young people were too appalled at the idea to participate, while others were excited in spite of their sense of guilt. For Anasuya, guilt was a new feeling. To have to hide something from her mothers felt simultaneously a bold and terrible thing to do. So she went with Hasha and some of the others, wading through the slippery passageways toward the place of the ancestors, plucking mussels from the walls and eating them. She shouted and laughed with the others but felt furtive inside. Still, there was nothing. No secret passage leading upward to a cave, let alone the cave they were seeking.

Hasha was disappointed. He had wanted to explore what it would be like to be alone, like the man in the story. What was it like to step outside the circle, to be one unto yourself, without people, and fish, and the sea? He grumbled and let himself be distracted by other pursuits.

While Hasha was busy with the other boys, learning to be men, chasing the great flocks of flying fish on their migrations up and down the coast, Anasuya went exploring again. She remembered seeing a place in the passageway—part of a wall— covered entirely with billik, a kind of seaweed with long fronds. So when the tide was low she went back to the place of the ancestors. She went slipping and sliding into the passageway they had explored, which smelled strongly of fish and brine, and found the place. She pushed aside the fronds; small carcasses of fish fell onto the floor. Ugh! Rotten fish. She found herself looking into a dark passage.

And yes, it led upward, just like the story, although the place it ended wasn't a round cave. It was more of a crack or slit close to the low ceiling of the passageway, into which she had to climb, scraping her knees, until she found herself in a place of near darkness. When her eyes adjusted she fought sudden claustrophobia. The passageway was below her—not far above her was the ceiling of the crevice. She was in the smallest space she'd ever been in. Surely this was not the cave they were seeking!

After a while she began to feel calmer, even a little bold. She wasn't really alone, the sea was just a little way down, and she could hear it thundering and booming in the passageways below. But she was hungry and thirsty—the search had taken longer than she thought.

Away from sun and sky, she couldn't tell how long. Perhaps it was time to start back.

But when she did, she met sea water just a few steps down the passage. Terror caught her then. The tide was rising. She needed to go back to the cramped little cave.

Just like the story, her mind told her. Sitting in the cave, she shook with fear. She felt around with her hands, but there were no more openings, only little cracks that let in some light. She must be close to the surface of the cliff, but there was no way out.

Would the sea come into the cave?

She closed her eyes and opened them again, but nothing had changed. The cave smelled faintly of brine, but it felt dry. Perhaps the water would not come in.

If only she had not listened to Hasha! She thought of him angrily, longingly, out there on the open sea.

The water did not come into the cave after all. But she was thirsty, and it was getting cold. She thought she heard the slow drip of water from somewhere above her. It was raining outside; she could hear the sound of rain and the sea, blurred into a roar like distant thunder.

She located the source of the dripping. Water dripped from a crevice on to a jutting rock, slid down the wall of the cave, and formed a tiny pool on a shelf of rock. She drank. It was slightly bitter (like the story, her mind said), but fresh.

There was a flash of lightning outside. The inside of the cave was suddenly lit up, although faintly. For a fraction of a second Anasuya saw her reflection in the little pool.

Her eyes, dark and frightened, her lips drawn back a little from her teeth. Anasuya alone, away from those she loved, away from sea and fish, sunlight and sky. She thought she heard her image calling to her. Then there was darkness again. She felt herself falling into nothing.

When she came to, the storm was over. She couldn't bear to stay in the cave. She waited in the passageway next to the black water, letting it lap at her ankles, comforted by its familiar language. Slowly the water retreated and Anasuya moved with it until she was climbing down, splashing untidily from the seaweed-fringed opening into the wider passage that led directly to the sea. Outside she took great, thankful lungfuls of air.

Anasuya did not tell anyone about her misadventure. Not even Hasha, especially not Hasha. She felt ashamed, frightened, every time she thought about what she had done. When, in the evenings, her mothers would tell the old stories, she would silently hope against hope that they wouldn't tell the story of the Cave of Delusion. But there were times when a child would ask for that story, or occasions when an elder was going on the last journey, and the story would have to be told. Anasuya would listen despite herself, and each time the story would cut her open, take her back to that place. For a long time she had nightmares about it, which began with one of her mothers telling the tale.

And she told Nirx that story.

Once there was a man of the Sunrise clan called Dara, who, escaping from a storm, crept into a crevice in a cliff and found himself in a passageway. He climbed up the narrow, twisting passage, fearful of the water smashing itself against the cliff face, sending waves into the crevice that pulled at his ankles. After some desperate climbing he found himself in a round cave, dark as night. It was high, beyond the reach of the water, and dry. So he sat himself down to wait for the storm and the tide to pass.

As he waited, he got thirsty. He was afraid of going back in case the passageway was filled completely with water. He started to feel around with his hands to see whether there was a way out of this cave other than the way he had come in. Pat, pat! went his hands on the walls. But there was nothing there. So the man wept a little and despite his fear and his thirst, fell asleep.

When he woke there was still seawater in the passageway but there was light seeping in through cracks in the ceiling, and he found, to his surprise, that there was a pool of rainwater in the middle of the cave's sandy floor. He cupped his hands in the pool and drank. He felt himself fill with water and gratitude. But later he tried to piss and he found he could not. His groin ached, and he realized that he was still thirsty, perhaps even more than before. So he went back to the pool and drank some more. And again, after a while he found he could not pass water, and the thirst came back. He did this five times or ten. Or maybe twenty.

Or maybe he's still doing it now, and that's the end of the story.

But if this is not the end, then listen. Next time Dara went to the water he did not drink, but looked into the pool instead.

He saw his reflection in the dim light.

And saw that he was the only one in the whole world. There was no sea, no fish, nothing except him in water that was not water. There was no athmis anywhere either.

"If only I exist," he asked his reflection in astonishment, "what am I, then?"

His image spoke:

"You are not yourself here, nor is this place what it seems. This water is not water but the drink of delusion. You must climb out of this cave and return to the sea, or you will stay in this place for eternity, alone."

In fear the man backed away and fell against the cave's walls. That woke him up, and he opened his eyes. He found that he was lying on a beach in the sunlight. He was not alone any more because the sea was whispering to him and the flying fish calling above his head, and in the water the seaphants were disporting themselves playfully. He sat up and his body ached with need. Looking down at his body he saw that what afflicted him was age and sickness, and what his body needed was the peace death brings. The sea was waiting to take him away to that death, but he had been afraid and had run away. He had thought he found shelter but he instead found the place where there is nothing at all, and only enough water to see your face in.

So he took a step toward the sea, and opened his eyes.

And he found himself on the longboat, with his brothers rowing him toward the reef where the leviathans waited. They had washed and anointed his body and had wrapped him in the wide, soft green leaves of the sailtrees. He found that his mind, too, had been washed of fear.

"You will step into a wider circle than any of us have known," said his brothers, kissing him. The water beat against the reef with a roaring, thundering sound.

They slid him gently out into the noisy sea. It seemed to him that within the confusion of the surf, the beating of the waves, was a current, swift and strong, pulling him along. Around him the waves rose up into the shapes of women; his mothers, he thought, as they leaned down to kiss him. And down he went into the green water, which was quiet underneath the violent perturbation of the surface. There at last were the great bulks, the waiting, open mouths, the tendrils that came snaking out toward him, drawing him in, accepting him, taking him home.

He opened his eyes.

Distances

Anasuya dreamed of blank spaces, little empty black spots like a sickness, eating away at the world. In her dream she kept trying to interpolate across the black regions, filling in a piece of sky here, a mesa there. It was a race against time, because the black spots were proliferating at an astonishing rate, and it was all she could do to keep up with them. Then she saw that they were eating her, too, because she could no longer see her hand in front of her face. She screamed and woke up.

She was lying on a couch in the art prep room. A low light was burning; the high window was full of stars. She sat up, wiped the edge of her mouth on the thick covers. Her scream echoed in her mind. But her hand was still there, visible, green, lightly freckled. And her art surrounded her as proof of the existence of the world. The night outside was not the black of ignorance: it was a friendly night filled with stars.

Time to take a few deep breaths.

The dream was no mystery. The blank spaces that had shown up in Nirx's mathematical space so long ago had become more profuse, and in some places, larger. So far Anasuya had been able to compensate for their presence through her skill at interpolating. She had discussed them often with Nirx. Nirx thought there might be some kind of degradation in the seed solution. The reconfiguration process could not compensate for that. But why not try making a new seed solution? Nirx shook her head thoughtfully. That would take months and equipment that was not available here.

The other option was sabotage.

Anasuya talked to Ahran about this. He was more inclined to believe that there was something wrong with the seed solution, but not for the reasons Nirx said.

"They're still keeping secrets from us," he told Anasuya. "I knew they would try to not share with us more than they had to. Now that the project is proceeding and we have as much of a stake in it as they do, they are trying to distract us from what we need to know."

Ahran told her that the part of the seed solution that had been given them was difficult to analyze. Of the thirteen ingredients, at least one was a complete mystery to the chemists. In all the mass analyses it came up as an unknown X, an emptiness, a black space, giving away its existence only through its weight. Kzoric insisted that the Temple chemists were doing the analysis all wrong, but there was, Ahran said, a smug look about her that infuriated him.

"Don't trust them, Anasuya," he told her. "They know you can interpolate through the blank areas in the holo. I feel—and Anhutip tell me if I'm wrong—that these blank spaces are a side-effect of their messing with the chemistry to keep the seed ingredients a secret. They don't care, as long as you can do what they want!"

But it was hard to be certain of the Tiranis' guilt in this matter. Nirx herself was beginning to look worried when Anasuya showed her how the black areas were proliferating.

"If they get any larger," Anasuya said, frowning, "I won't be able to interpolate."

She had been revisited several times by a feeling of panic, of time running out. Even though she had located how four-d space was immersed within hyperspace, the mapping process was tedious and slow. But this was the map all humankind had been waiting for; here were the paths upon which future ships would travel, faster than light, cheating time. Here, hyperspatial paths had to be located with hair's breadth precision in the neighborhood of familiar stars, connections made across the void between inhabited worlds, the future superhighways of humankind laid down. Future pathways for future lovers to meet. So Anasuya worked harder than she ever had, plotting and charting, resisting the temptation to explore the higher-dimensional spaces that truly fascinated her.

Vara seemed also to be acutely aware of time running out. During each meeting she seemed more anxious, her eyes bright with urgency. Her mouth opened around words that made soft echoes in Anasuya's mind. *I have no time. Take this gift. Take space. Make art.*

And the art was coming into being, piece by piece. Between sessions in the amnion, Anasuya gave herself up to her creation, forgetting to eat and sleep, distractedly accepting food and drink from the ever attentive Amas. Working in a frenzy, sometimes well into dawn, Anasuya would sometimes forget whether she was engaged in studying and re-building hyperspace or creating art. There were resemblances. Only, here, in her art work, she could bring out the beauty of the full sthanas. She had that freedom, at least. She had been thinking for some time that Vara must have been brought forth from these most mysterious regions of meta-reality.

It was in the art prep room that she slept, on the broad couch. Here she would lie sometimes, lost in reverie, staring unseeingly out of the window into the night sky. An idea, a memory, or something Vara said would step quietly into her mind, and she would jump up, alive and eager. Erase that last thing she had done! Forget temporal linearity — how to simulate non-linearity in time? Have the holo go back and forth between scenes, show scenes morphing, but not as you would expect if time flowed only one way…

Anasuya hadn't gone home in a long time. When she went home, next, only Marko and Silaf were there. The House felt empty, her mates strange. She missed Palanik but he was away. Coming back soon, Anasuya. Why don't you stay? Marko entreated her while Silaf tapped out a soft rhythm on her gwi lover's bones and looked at her in that unfathomable way. Anasuya felt that something at home had shifted, was changed, but she couldn't understand it. What she wanted was not here. She wanted, needed, to get back to her work. She could rest later. After a day home, she was restless; she said her goodbyes and stepped out into a cool dawn.

It was then, in the half-light and silence, that she made a discovery. Scratching her arm lightly, she looked down at it. Where she had had a light scattering of freckles on the inside of her left forearm was a patch of brown skin as big as her thumbnail. She touched it like someone feeling a loose tooth, glancing at her almost-bare body in consternation. But as far as she could see, it was only in that one spot where the soliforms that gave her body its green tint, that kept the spiroforms alive in her blood — the soliforms were dying.

In terror she looked around her at the world. She could still see the mathematics of it — in the outline of the mesas against a red sky, the semi-regular spiraling of the walkways as they rose up the hill. Order and beauty as she had known them since her fifth year. But wasn't there a smudging here, a blurring there, little regions of opacity? Little blind spots, hardly noticeable until now.

She knew, then, that the black spots in hyperspace were because of her. She was going blind, slowly, losing the mathematical sight that had made her what she was.

She swayed, righted herself. In the amnion, which created an environment that enhanced and magnified her skill, the blind spots were more noticeable. No wonder she hadn't caught on at once.

She took a long, shuddering breath. She wanted to look at herself more closely, to see whether there were other brown patches. But she did not want to return home and have to explain. She didn't want anyone to know what was happening to her...

Anasuya, without her athmis. She couldn't imagine that. She thought: if I don't get it back, I want to die.

Once, before she left the sea, Anasuya had seen a brown man.

She and Lata had ventured out of the underwater forests close to shore—riding their reed raft they had made their way across the bay toward the less dense forests of kiputi weeds. Here a broad, sandy ridge rose from the sea bed, studded with great boulders. The sea had carved smooth, round caves in the stone, from which the men peered and waved. Their longboats lay like plump eels on the sand. The brown man sat on his haunches atop a rock, staring at the water.

Among the green folk the brown man looked odd. He looked ill. Anasuya wasn't sure if she should stare at him. When she did, he turned dark, sorrowful eyes upon her until she looked away with a shudder. She asked Lata who he was.

"I do not know what wind or wave brought him here," she said. "He speaks our tongue and claims he was born out of our wombs. He says he fell sick in his eighteenth year and was given to the leviathans, but a wave took him beyond that to the open sea. It is the rogue wave, the Trickster wave, my dear, that you must always be wary of because it will take you far away. He says he sailed across the sea, and then the land. He was away so long that the sea washed out of him, and he turned brown like the sand. Now he is back, and even though he swims in the sea, the sea will not swim in him again."

"Will he die?"

"How can he die a second time? How can I say? The old men take care of him and feed him, and one of them remembers him when he was alive. But he is only part of what he was. A strange thing, who cannot claim his old name, because that was given to the leviathans when he died."

The next time Anasuya saw the brown man, the season of the rains had just begun. She saw him through the skeins of rain, perched on the same rock. But this time Hasha was with him. Hasha saw her and waved. She had been seeing him less frequently lately. What was he doing with the stranger? What were they talking about?

Hasha told her the next time they met. In the green darkness, under the wind trees, on a sloping sandy shore, she lay against him and heard the story. What the brown man had told Hasha was that Hasha's visions were true—there really were stone places in sandy oceans, where the stone people lived. He had been to such places and seen things with his own eyes! There were vast boats that ferried people across the starry expanses. The elders had not told Hasha the truth. In the intimate darkness, in the silence before the wind trees started their wet, wild thrashing, their wind-making, Hasha told her what he wanted to do. He wanted to cross the marsh forest until the ground felt more and more solid under his feet, until the ground became stone. There he would make a boat that would sail him over the land and find out what the world had to say to him there.

"Don't say such things," she said, frightened. "It's the Trickster wave in your mind, Hasha! Don't trust it!"

But he wouldn't listen.

"Come with me," he begged her. "We'll go over the shore and beyond, where the marshgrove trees end. You're not like the others, you see things that are true but not obvious to ordinary sound and sight. I want to see the places in my visions. Come with me!"

She could have told him that there were others whose gift wasn't easy to share. Her own gift was a fairly common one; there were other forms the gift took that were stranger than his. But it was in Hasha's eyes that the athmis burned most strongly. She took his face between her hands and kissed his mouth and felt the youth, the wildness of him. And she felt her whole being answer that wildness.

But she couldn't leave Lata behind, betray her, discard the love and learning like a used shell.

She believed then that if she was steadfast, Hasha would be forced to stay, that she could keep him from the Trickster. There would be more of the crazy talk that quickened her blood, the promise of the next meeting under the wind trees, and the next and the next.

But she couldn't hold him, nor could the sea.

It started with the disappearance of the brown man. Nobody saw him leave, but men on a longboat quite some distance away thought they saw a brown fish as big as a man, swimming toward the reef under which the leviathans lay. The fish would swim, drift, then swim again. It was like no other fish they had seen; an elder thought it might be a curiously pigmented sunfish. Sunfish have limbs and live near the surface and often swim in this manner. It did not occur to anybody that the brown man had left to make of himself the final gift. Only when the men searched for him and couldn't find him did they realize what had happened.

There was talk about whether the leviathans would accept his gift, whether it was a noble thing the man had done, or a foolish one. But Hasha did not say anything; he stayed at the edge of the gathering, looking unusually subdued.

Three days later Hasha vanished.

He didn't make of himself a sacrifice to the leviathans. The last person to see him saw him going the other way. Over land, not sea. A small, determined figure, high up on a distant cliff, his back to them all. Walking away from the sea.

Mourning on her reed raft while Lata dived for fish, Anasuya heard the waves lapping: never come home, never come home. Hasha will never come home.

Lata tried to help her understand her grief.

"Even our feelings have patterns," she said to Anasuya. "The mind, too, is a heaving sea. Understanding the harmonies of the mind, the soul that holds the athmis…now that would be a great thing!

"I see greatness for you, my Anasuya. You will be a singer of the harmonies on festival nights, in the winter caves. Your songs will be carved on the walls where our ancestors' poems are written. But before that time comes you must understand many things. Let me tell you now, a story."

It was an old story, but comforting to hear again:

This story tells of the three women who were taken by the Trickster.

It was the season of the rains. Great storm clouds moved over the sea, loosing rain over the heaving waters. The sea became opaque with agitation, and the great underwater forests swayed wildly with the currents. So the women retreated into caves and other shelters like the men.

The three women had gone to tend to a man who was ill, over at the Sunset clan men's place. A longboat had come to fetch them, and although it had trouble navigating, the women arrived safely and bent to their task. They had to tell if the man was truly dying, in which case the men must row him to the leviathans' before he became a corpse, or whether he would recover. They tended him for three days and three nights, but he did not get better. Let me make of myself the Gift, while I can, he told them. Let my mates take me to the place where the Great Ones wait.

So they kissed his brow and said the ritual farewells.

The storm paused in its violence; from a break in the clouds, the sun peered out, gilding everything. The watching women squinted in the sudden light, saw the longboat make its way swiftly to the patch of green sea, the shallow place under which the leviathans had their dwelling. Thinking they had best return while the

Distances

storm was paused, they asked for the loan of a reed raft rather than wait until the men made ready another longboat. The men gave them a raft, but with anxious warnings that the women did not heed.

So they clambered aboard the raft and raised the small sail and began to steer their way toward the distant shore.

Then the storm broke once more. A great tower of rain came down from the sky and obliterated everything, and there was a flash of lightning, followed very quickly by thunder. As the men ran to shelter one of them paused on the sodden beach, shading his eyes to look after the women. In a gap in the rain he saw two things that astounded him. First, a great, green wave moving swiftly toward them from the open sea. Then, the raft with the three women, out on the sea, facing the wave. And the sail was dropped, and the three women were standing on the raft, riding it through the furrows of the sea, their arms held out in anticipation *toward* the wave.

And that was the last that was seen of the women.

Later the men in the longboat returned, having given not one but two to the leviathans. They were weary and spent, and the boat much damaged by the storm, but two of them took another boat shoreward to search for the women, because they could not believe that the women had gone around the island to meet the wave — but they did not find what they sought. So the story that the young man told of what he saw was taken to be the truth, and it was said that the wave was the Trickster wave.

The legend goes that the wave took the three women away to the farthest shores of the Sky Sea itself, the place from which the leviathans had come. But others say this is nonsense, that the women went under the wave to where the leviathans live, but remain alive to this day, serving the Great Ones and combing their sea-weed-encrusted heads with combs of bone. They say that the Three Women, when invoked during a storm, will bring the boat to calm waters. Some men claim to have seen, during the rainy season, the Three Women out in their raft.

The Trickster does not always appear as a wave, but might take its form as the underwater current that tugs you away from home, or the mad wind that springs up out of a clear sky and sweeps you and your raft away.

Some stories talk about the Trickster and the leviathans having made a pact with each other in times now forgotten…

They say the leviathans came from the stars and that part of them still yearns for the great journeys in the wide, empty spaces. That part, that wandering, far-seeing, restless piece of the leviathan soul, is not content with living within the interlocking circles of Sagara. So the leviathans made a pact with the Trickster that every once in a while such fragments of the soul would go out into the wider world and fulfill this wanderlust. In early times there were no prohibitions against some people going away from Sagara and then coming back. In fact they held some position of honor. But later when some of them brought foreigners with them, who wanted to dive down into the ocean depths to find out who or what the leviathans were, or break in other ways the sacred rituals of the Sagaran people, then stepping outside the circle began to be frowned upon. Those who returned alone were taken in, even if they had lost their athmis, but such things were not spoken well of and certainly never encouraged.

Who is the Trickster? It is that part of the sea, the soul, the universe, that plays tricks, deludes and ultimately takes by surprise. It is the one that does not play by the rules. So a sudden wind, a treacherous wave or undertow is an aspect of the Trickster.

In the silence after the story, Anasuya thought of Hasha walking over miles of the unimaginable land. Lata said:

"You have much to do here, my Anasuya. Promise me, you will guard your soul from the Trickster."

And Anasuya promised.

But even before she could finish mourning for Hasha, the unexpected happened.

Just a handful of time later, Lata fell sick beyond her ability to cure herself. She had been bitten by a giant lamprey while fishing underwater. The poison had gone deep into her body, even though she had cut the bite and let herself bleed from it. The wound wouldn't heal, and she lay in a fever on the reed raft, muttering to herself; no herb or weed would bring her relief. Anasuya had hardly any time to think the word "death."

Suddenly their raft was overrun with her other mothers, who wept and embraced the dying woman and listened to her last recitation. "In beauty I was born," Lata said in a ragged whisper, "and to beauty I go." She kissed the stricken Anasuya and told her: "Remember what I have taught you, dearest of daughters! May you always be within the circle." Then she spoke the names of all her sisters and lovers and birth-children.

In the fog-shrouded morning the longboat came, rowed by quiet men like graven images, and Lata was placed in it tenderly, lovingly, by the women, while Anasuya wept. Lata raised a hand weakly in farewell; the boat slipped rapidly away. Anasuya dropped into the water, not heeding the calls of her other mothers, following the longboat even though she knew she would never catch up with it.

Afterward, exhausted and too weak for tears, she lay in the water, watching the boat move out of sight. She imagined the leviathans waiting, suspended in the water like drowned islands, encrusted with barnacles and weeds. The leviathans: gift-givers and life-takers, seeding the children of the sea with the athmis, the green sperm, and at the end of each life, bringing the swift death that completes the circle. Lata was gone: she was in the leviathans' belly, in their flesh and bones, and ultimately she would be the spiroforms, the seaweed, the sea itself. And that was no comfort.

That night she persuaded her other mothers to let her stay on the raft alone. Women had done that, for mourning and for meditation, for composing new songs. Her mothers embraced her and let her go.

She lay on the raft in tears, mourning first Lata, then Hasha, then Lata again. The sea was quiet, the waves lapping gently against the raft. There was a breathless calm, as that which comes before a storm. She raised her head and looked at the moonlit sea. Was there a raft out there, in the far waters? Was she imagining the Three Women, beckoning to her?

And the Trickster wave came roaring into her mind.

Night. A storm, an anchor cut with a fishbone knife, and the reed island was free. It roamed out into the open sea with Anasuya clinging to it. She survived the beating of wind and waves, the crashing of the angry sea. She saw the clouds scatter and the two little moons appear, silvering and calming the sea; she saw the stars reflected and distorted in the water.

Dawn brought a sparse catch of fish and hunger—and the great surprise of a vast bulk over the horizon. She thought it was a leviathan surfacing, but it was only a very large boat with strange, brown people in it, dry as bone even in the midst of the sea. They leaned over the edge of the ship, shouting and gesticulating. Someone threw a long rope down to her. She looked at her raft; the reeds were already separating, their lashings damaged by the storm. She didn't know what to do. If she remained on the raft she would die, and it would be a gift wasted, not a true death. She looked up at the rope, put her hands around it, and began to climb slowly and painfully. The strange people were reaching for her arms, pulling her onto the broad, flat deck. She was in a terrifyingly unfamiliar place, surrounded by dry bone people. The world tilted; she saw mast, and sail, and sky — and she fell. Then time seemed to run very fast, and there was a long period of terror and confusion.

When she emerged from that time, she was still on the ship. She was in a strange cave with pleasing mathematical regularities. There was a ghost-like person, someone thin and pale, speaking in her language but saying the words all wrong, and confined space, walls everywhere. The incredible variety of artificial harmonies mimicking the natural ones: the plain rectangular geometry of the cabin, the carefully skewed symmetry of an abstract painting, the perfection of the circular bowl that held her tea. It broke upon her consciousness that here were things made by use of mathematical harmonies. All made-things, a shameless exploitation of the patterns and relationships taught to her by Lata! In the shock of it all she discovered that some of the things were beautiful. Other things were mostly bewildering: clothes, plates, cutlery, strange foods. But most difficult of all was the throat-clogging dryness of everything, as though the air itself had been sucked of moisture.

Then, after the sea journey there was another one, over land desiccated beyond imagination, with her mouth gasping for breath and her neck-slits gritty and clamped shut. She thought of Hasha, but nobody in her group of travelers knew of any other person of Sagara who had come to the dry land. Maybe he would be in the great City where they were going—at some time or other, everyone who was not taken by the Nameless Goddess of the desert found their way to the City.

On the journey she tried to recall the sea, the place that was her home, her guiding spirit, her sanctum. But all the memory gave her was guilt and loss. There was no comfort in it, no promise of wholeness, no reminder of who she was, because she was turning into something else. She had stepped out of the circle, and in doing so had betrayed all of them, Lata and her other mothers, and the sea itself. But there was no going back.

Now, years from that day, she drew her shift over the bare brown spot on her arm, and remembered. And thought: the sea dies in me.

Anasuya went to a healer. She had heard about him from some of the Temple chemists. This healer was an expert on the kinds of rare sicknesses one got after too much cavorting with foreign tribes during festival season. Once he had been employed by the Temple of Two Lovers to minister to the ones sick with love, or with the things that sometimes came with it; now he was old, lived in near-seclusion at the other end of the City, and rarely saw people.

Anasuya's meeting had come about after a long search and many exchanges of cryptic messages. She went in secret, slipping out of the Temple doors one night, her robe about her shoulders. Once clear of the Temple, she put the robe on properly: wore the sleeves and even the veil, which was only used when a sandstorm was nigh. She felt awkward and restricted in her clothes and kept having to remember not to push up her sleeves. A few people stared at her on the walkways and in the speeders but nobody recognized her.

The healer's room was high inside a mesa; a round window gave a panoramic view of the City at night. On the shelves there were tiny nematodes, and solutions containing various protozoans, and jars and jars of microscopic stone and metal machines that hummed. The healer was a small, lugubrious man, sporting a skullplate and cheek-plate of burnished metal in which she could see distorted images of her face and the room. Looking at him was oddly disturbing, because it was as though he wasn't really there. He examined her blood and said that the spiroforms were still thriving, but he could not say whether the soliforms would continue to die or not. "Your kind is rare in our city," he said apologetically. "Your body ecology is mysterious to us. Since the War two hundred years ago, many of us cannot maintain our internal ecology without the help of these tiny machines. It is all I can offer—but I cannot guarantee that they will work on you." He set a jar of silvery liquid before her. She shuddered, shook her head, and took her leave.

Distances

She worried and fretted and examined her body several times a day. For a while, nothing changed, and then, a few days later, there was a brown spot on her knee. She knew, then, that she was doomed.

In the amnion, the regions of blindness were becoming larger every session. She lived in terror that Ahran would figure it out. Sometimes she thought he was looking at her in a puzzled way. Other times she was almost certain Nirx knew, that a casual glance sent Anasuya's way during a difficult interpolation meant that Nirx suspected. She couldn't bear anyone to find out, least of all those who were close to her. But the history of tension between the Tiranis and the Temple chemists shielded her. Every day there was a quarrel or two that Nirx or an increasingly frustrated Ahran would have to try their best to control.

"We need to finish this project," Nirx told Anasuya one day. Her hair was coming apart from the coiled braid she usually wore; her face looked pinched and tired. "I am afraid of what might happen…"

Kzoric went about her work, scowling. Turel and Hiroq had apparently had an argument, because she was red-nosed and quiet, and he looked miserable. Neither spoke to the other, although Anasuya sometimes caught Hiroq looking at Turel across the room, as she bent over her work. The longing in his eyes was painful to see.

Anasuya covered up her fear by burying herself in work and art. Outwardly she tried to maintain a detached, cheerful demeanor, but it didn't entirely fool

Nirx or Ahran. On different occasions each of them had asked her if something was wrong. Each time Anasuya shook her head and smiled and claimed fatigue, although Ahran's concern had brought tears to her eyes. She had to turn away and busy herself so he wouldn't see.

She painted over the brown patches, at least in the regions visible to others. Ironically, the green unguents and dyes that had become so fashionable among the people of the City not long ago came in useful now. She had also changed her manner of dress, although not so drastically that anyone would notice. Now the cooler weather was on its way; in a month or so there would be the time of the festivals and the scant rain of the desert. Once she would have looked forward to all that; now she felt dead to the pleasures of the world.

It was hard to believe that so many months had passed since the coming of the Tiranis. They were going to leave soon; they weren't even going to wait for the season of the festivals. The ship to Tirana would be leaving in less than a month, and they would have to be on it.

In the amnion, Vara had begun to seem a little less distinct each time. Her eyes had grown larger, more nocturnal, as though she, too, was having difficulty seeing Anasuya across whatever barriers separated them. Here, in the blessed darkness of the amnion, Anasuya could let her sorrow run like a river. Here she could ask Vara in her mind, with all the anguish she had to otherwise conceal: why is this happening to me? Will I see you, the next time I'm here?

To which Vara had no reply but an answering sadness in her eyes.

And again, the urgent message: *No Time. Make art.*

So Anasuya worked in a frenzy, as though every day was the last day of her life. The day came when she could no longer ignore the blind spots in her mathematical vision, even when she was out of the amnion. She stopped going home to her mates; she could not bear the thought of their finding out, their sympathy. All the time she was in the grip of a passionate desperation. She mapped hyperspace with a single-minded intensity that astonished the Tiranis and Temple chemists alike, and she created fantastic holos in which manic rage melded with art to create the poetry of new and strange geometries. Now as art and hyperspatial mathematics began to reinforce each other more than they ever had, she sensed something building up inside her, something crystallizing out of formlessness, becoming ready to be born. It was time to finish her ultimate work of art. All her earlier creations had been leading up to this. She had been dabbling with it, filling in a corner here, a piece there, but there was no more time for play. She was filled with a breathless urgency, a sense that the world itself was standing still, waiting for her masterpiece. All the hints and glimpses she had had of this work in the depths of mathematical space, in her dreams, coalesced into a vast, clear vision. In a holocube so huge that spectators would have to walk between its interlocking chambers, her art slowly took form.

Meanwhile hyperspace continued to reveal its exotic topography. The analysis room rang with debates and celebrations, the waxing and waning of hope, the warring of the two factions and the peace-making. Anasuya spent hours editing the holos with Nirx peering over her shoulder. It was getting harder and harder to interpolate across the black spaces. Sometimes, leaping across them gave her a sensation of vertigo, as though she was jumping across a chasm. But she trusted to blind luck and Vara's guiding hand, and so far she had succeeded.

At last Nirx announced that only one or two more sessions in the amnion were needed.

"We have just enough of the original solution left," she said. "Except for the seed sample we have left with you. But we have enough information to excite the experimentalists and technologists. After this last session or two, we will consolidate our data and prepare for our return. It is not inconceivable, my Lord Chemist, that if we see each other next, one of us would have traveled through hyperspace to meet the other."

Ahran inclined his head courteously, but he didn't say much. Anasuya knew that the temple chemists were still having trouble with the seed. Ahran had told her that the identity of the unknown ingredient was still uncertain. The latest tests had revealed that if there was such a thing in the brew, it was in a very small quantity. Barely a contamination, barely above detectable levels. This contradicted what the chemists had found in earlier tests, but Kzoric insisted there was nothing to worry about.

Nirx's quiet joy was mixed with a darker, more complex emotion. Anasuya found her, once, in a thoughtful, almost melancholy mood, sitting in the dark in the nearly deserted refectory. "It's the weight of the responsibility," Nirx said with a sigh. "There are times when I don't feel equal to the burden."

She took a sip of nectar, sighed again. "Tell me, Anasuya, why is it we must seek answers? Why can't we be content with our ignorance? I have given my life for this work. Others have quite literally given their lives, and with something of such importance, I know there will be more sacrifices to come. Has it been worth it? Who can tell?" She looked at Anasuya. "You have done this marvelous thing, changed humanity's fate. How do you feel?"

How did she feel? Anasuya could not comprehend the enormity of what she had done. Yes, she had opened the doors to the stars, but they were still distant suns to her. What she feared most she could not put into words. She looked around her. The refectory was almost deserted; it was late evening, and the lights were glowing along the walls. The mathematical harmonies were muted, blurred, as though something was washing them out. Anasuya swallowed hard. "I don't know," she told Nirx. "I don't know what I feel."

In her last session in the amnion, she found that she was flying nearly blind. The darkness had eaten away at hyperspace almost completely. She wept into the brew, knowing it was all over. When the faintly visible structures of hyperspace began to come apart, she saw that Vara was no longer there. All there was, was a shadow, a ghost. A dark opening that opened and collapsed, which might have been Vara's mouth, speaking.

Outside she couldn't help it; she cried. Ahran held her, unmindful that she was dripping with water and chemicals. Nirx patted her shoulder.

"Don't worry, the solution's completely degraded," Nirx said. "But we have all we need, Anasuya! We have won!"

But Anasuya would not give in so easily. She spent many hours painfully plotting and interpolating at the holo, checking each change against the possibility of error, correcting errors as they arose. She took earlier holos with similar features and did cross-comparisons. Ahran and Nirx watched her, amazed. But she was unaware of them. If she couldn't finish this, she would not be able to finish her art, which lay almost complete up in the art room.

And when she put in the last check, the last change, and saved the information and leaned back with a sigh and a suddenly aching back, the room cheered. She got up in confusion, realizing only now that she had had an audience for all these hours.

The next day Anasuya's own masterpiece was completed. She had wanted to sculpt her Muse out of mathematics and light, and she had done it. Here were the depths of the sthanas, space and time tangled in non-linear whirlpools; here, pricking out of the darkness were dazzling mosaics so intricate that the viewer might find her gaze falling into them for eternity. In this topography there were hints of Vara, these the planes of her face, the proud crag of her nose, the marks of old sorrow in the gullies and rifts of her cheeks. It was not at all a literal rendering of Vara's face, although if you turned in certain directions in certain places, you would think you saw a slender woman walking slowly and with dignity along the crest of a low hill, picking her way among an intricacy of strange attractors. If you wandered another way you would see the twin pools of her eyes, fringed by green growth, beckoning and mysterious, brimming with the errors of some lost, misspent youth. Here was the crinkled rose of her mouth, parted with words that formed and hung and dissipated in the mist. Here were hyperbolic delights of the body and the mind, the seaweed forest in all its variety, silver quickfish darting in the shallows, their ripples breeding complexity upon complexity until they dissipated or turned into tidal waves. In places there were hidden currents, yearning toward the open sea like functions toward asymptotes, where eternity waited with open jaws. This at last was the path, the way, the map of Vara.

Looking at it after it was over, a thought came into Anasuya's mind: I will never create again. She rejected the thought almost as soon as it was formed, but it left a lingering feeling of deep dismay.

That evening people thronged before the holo. It had been set up in the atrium for public viewing. They came in waves from the City, they came in little rivulets from the passageways of the Institute, from its round stone chambers. Her mates came, embraced her, walked through the display, wide-eyed, and looked at her again with new eyes. The Tiranis paused in their packing and came to see it. They walked around and in it and stared, and marveled.

Late that evening, the Master came. He gazed at the holo in silence, going around it, staring at it with manic intensity as it played out: time and space tangled in wonderful geometries. Anasuya watched the colors wash the space around the holo. It was dark and quiet but for that and the Master's muffled grunts. The crowds had gone.

The Master turned to Anasuya and ducked his hideous head. His chest shook. Anasuya backed away, half-frightened, but the Master came up to her and looked into her face. She saw her reflection in his deep, shadowed eyes, below the ridge of his cranial plate. He passed his tongue against his teeth. A drop of blood trickled down his chin. His eyes were brimming with tears.

"So I have lived to see this..." he whispered. "This is what I was waiting for! This is why Anhutip breathed you into the world! Why did you throw away time all these years and days? Playing with things you know nothing about! Sending ships across the voids for the foreigners! Why didn't you create art before? Instead... Oh, what have you done to me, Anasuya!"

He turned from her and staggered away, one hand held to his face. She stared at his retreating figure in horror. What had she meant to him; what had she done to him with her art? She didn't want to have anything to do with him. She felt sick.

She sat down on the bench and passed her hand over her eyes. In the vast hall her breathing seemed magnified.

"Is this the new sthanas—hyperspace?" Amas said to her, coming up through the darkness and silence. He had been standing shyly behind the crowds all evening, staring over their shoulders and marveling. His face brimmed with awe and pride. "Is this the poetry you set out to find?"

She tried to explain to him that the Tirani project and her art were two separate but related things, but that only confused him. "I will bring you tea," he said tenderly, proudly. He went off into the darkness of the atrium.

Anasuya arranged herself on the bench, grateful for the quiet and the emptiness, stretching her aching arms behind her. She felt completely exhausted, too spent for tears. She closed her eyes.

But before sleep came, someone else came up to her, faithful Amas with his bowl of steaming tea. She sat up, only half awake and a little annoyed. She reached for the bowl but Amas held it away from her. His eyes were large with tears. His wet mouth moved without sound. The bowl fell from his hands and broke with a reverberating crash, sending a scalding wave over the floor. Anasuya lifted her feet out of reach, but now she saw that Amas was falling slowly into the pool of tea, his hands reaching out before him, folding up under his body. She knelt by him, suddenly awake, and raised his dripping head. He turned toward her, his eyes filled with tears. He tried to say something. She bent closer, her heart pounding, her hand smoothing his cheek.

"…said it was boundaries…make us who we are… wrong, you did wrong to…remove boundaries…didn't trust…so I tasted it first…"

She shouted for help. Footsteps came running out of the darkness; hands lifted Amas' limp body away from her.

"The tea was poisoned," she whispered in horror. The novice who was trying to soothe her looked at her without comprehension, but one of the lesser masters understood. The novice was sent to get one of the chemists. Anasuya left the atrium and went out into the night, not knowing where she was going. She shivered. She had forgotten her cloak.

She turned back into the portals of the Temple, went up the stairway to the empty art room that had

Distances

become her home and huddled on the couch and wept, waiting sleeplessly for dawn.

At dawn they found the Master hanging from the long rope in the middle of the atrium. A ray of sunlight caught his skull-plate and imbued it with crimson fire as he swung one way, then another, endlessly, like a strand of seaweed caught between two eddies.

The funeral was over, the ceremonies all done. The Tiranis had stayed out of courtesy, but now it was time for them to leave. The Temple's new Master, a quiet, grave woman with an agate faceplate, had invited the guests to stay for the first great City Festival, when three great migrating tribes, Ghoomin, peri-human, and gwi, would cross paths, set up camp within the city itself, and delight the inhabitants with their trade and tricks. But the ship would not wait. Besides, there was a universe out there waiting for the answers they had obtained.

On the last day there was a muted celebration. The Tiranis were seated with the Temple team they had worked with, and fine food and drinks were served by novices. Turel and Hiroq were inseparable, as they had been these many days, with their impending farewell hanging over them. The conventions of the Lattice of Tirana would not allow Hiroq to stay; Turel had too much she would leave behind if she were to go with him. Today Kzoric was loud and more than a little drunk. She sat next to Anasuya, leaning toward her at intervals, laughing when Anasuya frowned at her or leaned away.

"Wait until the hyperspatial cruisers come, little green girl! Then your people will come into their glory. They'll be sung all over the galaxy! There will be a little green fish in every pool!"

Across the table Nirx frowned at Kzoric. The Temple's novices began passing around calabashes of special maraquel wine, at which the conversation died to murmurs of amazement. Maraquel fruit was rare, growing around only a few oases in the desert. The tree fruited once in a hundred years. The wine was reserved for the most special occasions; locked in a cellar below the Master's chambers, the last time it was brought out had been over twenty years ago.

Kzoric drank three gulps before she died. Death came swiftly to Vachkal, a young Temple chemist, as well. First there was the horror, then paralysis, then the end. Nirx, about to put the calabash against her lips, stopped herself in time and saved two others by dashing their calabashes from their hands. Anasuya saw Amas' rigid deathface before her eyes — she stood up and began to scream: "It's poisoned! The Master poisoned it before he killed himself!"

So before the final farewell, there were additional funeral ceremonies and the packing of Kzoric's body in ice for the long journey home. Poor Kzoric finally had her freedom. Nirx seemed to have aged years; her hands had developed a trembling she could not control.

At the final goodbye, just before the flyer took the Tiranis to the spaceport in Tilfax, Hiroq and Turel embraced for the last time. Climbing up the steps of the flyer, Hiroq said brokenly to Turel:

"It should have been me who died, not Kzoric, or that poor young man. To stay here with you…"

"We are dead already," Turel wept. "When the ship leaves, we will be dead."

"No, no," Nirx told her, smiling, although she looked very tired. "Perhaps when our ship docks on Tirana you'll be already on your way through hyperspace to meet us. Isn't it for this very purpose that we have worked?"

But Turel kept crying. Panjar came and held her. Turel sobbed against Panjar, violently, copiously, as though she would drown in her own tears. Anasuya, watching, felt her eyes prickling.

Nirx pushed Hiroq gently into the shuttle. She came to stand before Anasuya.

"My poor, dear child! It began badly. How it will end I don't know, but your Master and the two who followed him were the first victims."

"And Amas," Anasuya said.

"And your Amas," agreed Nirx. She reached up, touched Anasuya's cheek. Then she was gone.

The next day, Anasuya wandered like a ghost around the Temple, avoiding the crowds that came to see her work and pay homage. During the mid-day hiatus she sat on the circular bench in the atrium, alone, and thought about what she would have to do. How much time did she have before she was expected to enter the amnion again? Ahran was still busy studying the seed solution. She must leave before they could find out she was of no use to them now.

She wondered whether the Master would have done what he did had he known that her mathematical sight was gone. What had he seen when he looked at her masterpiece? What had he seen when he had looked at her, Anasuya?

As for Amas...

No, she could not bear to think about him just yet.

That night Ahran found her in her old art room.

"The seed solution," he said angrily. "I've just begun to understand what happened. When we first did tests on it, it worked fine with the micros. We didn't suspect anything. Then we began the analysis. Remember the unknown ingredient? It gradually degraded until there was nothing left? As you can imagine, the seed is nothing without it. It doesn't work. The chemistry is completely different."

He paused for breath.

"They cheated us, at the end," he said. "Here's my idea how. When I talked to Hiroq once, he told me that the ship that first discovered hyperspace had traces of exotic matter on it. He said the remnants were dimensionally unstable; they tunneled very quickly back into hyperspace. You remember the tensor fields you discovered in the sthanas? They were matter fields—exotic matter fields? Well, I think the Tiranis actually captured some of this matter from that experimental ship. They must have had some of that in the seed solution. Maybe it was protected in the solution by some kind of molecular cage that degrades unless it is continually chemically strengthened. Which, of course, they didn't tell us!"

"I can't believe Nirx would have cheated us," Anasuya said. "It must have been the others, Ahran! Kzoric, or Vishk…"

Ahran shook his head doubtfully. "How will we ever know how much they lied to us? I knew there was a missing X in the equation, Anasuya! That was it."

"But we have the earlier holos," she said, wanting to comfort him.

Secretly she felt a vast relief. If the seed solution had worked, she would have to go back into the amnion very soon. It would not have taken Ahran long to realize that Anasuya was going mathematically blind. Still, she would have to leave here before they assigned her to another project. A thought came to her that perhaps the exotic ingredient in the brew had hastened her blindness. There was no way to know. She shivered. She looked at his kindly, aging, angry face, and wished she could tell him everything.

"Yes, we have the holos," Ahran said. "The engineers are all over them like an invasion of roll-bugs. We have the map of hyperspace—and fourteen years to develop the technology. Which is not a very long time, considering we don't have expertise in deep-space experimental propulsion systems, like the Tiranis do."

He smiled at her, squeezed her shoulder.

"But we have you," he said. "And they don't."

Anasuya nodded, unable to speak. He patted her on the head and left the room.

Some days later, Anasuya was standing in the dim emptiness of the atrium, watching the play of light. A last red ray moved slowly up the great stone walls as the sun set. It hit a mirror set high in the wall and became two rays. One entered a suspended prism and created a band of color on the opposite wall. Watching, Anasuya realized she could no longer sense the harmonies of reflection and refraction, the relationships between angles. She was completely blind. She would have to recall the formulas, to spell it out like a child. She ran her hands over her face and felt the first, slightly itchy spot on her cheek. She shivered suddenly and remembered the dark boat coming over the water, through the mist, coming to take Lata away. She thought: the sea dies in me. She left the empty hall and went out into the alien night.

Outside, the City was lit up for the first great Festival of the year. The peri-humans had set up camp in the plazas that were reserved for this purpose, and there were lanterns floating everywhere and laughter and the chatter of strange languages. The gwi sat atop the mesas, mating and slapping their wings, descending only to trade with the City folk, the Ghoomin, and the peri-humans. There was music and the swirling of robes, the stamping of feet, while great holographic displays rippled across the plazas. Anasuya walked past the little trade-stops where the three species exchanged goods: gwi brought wing-feathers, pretty rocks that the City's gem experts valued, rare worms and herbs for the ecologists, while the peri-humans, their lean, long-snouted faces rapt as they bargained, brought cloth from far-off Napia, wool from their herds of laghoris, and other odd things picked up on their nomadic journeys. All this they exchanged for technoware, mathematical art holos, and jars of the tiny, invisible metal machines for which the City was famous. There were also the Ghoomin, the tribe of wandering humans to which Silaf had once belonged, their eyes aslant in their dark faces underneath white turbans, showing their skill with juggling knives, carving for the tourists mysterious idols of stone. The Ghoomin bards told stories of their great trek through lands ruined by the War two hundred years ago, and there was much mingling and gossiping, fleshing out the news from far lands. None of it meant anything to Anasuya, who wandered dazedly through the crowds under the bright, floating lanterns, not knowing where to go, until sheer exhaustion led her to a laghori pen. The smell was extraordinary, pungent and strong, and the animals themselves lay in great, huddled masses, their long-haired bodies steaming slightly in the cooling air. Drawn to them by something she could not explain to herself, she stumbled on something cool and coarse—a mat, she realized, woven out of laghori wool, and fell against the body of a sleeping beast. The creature woke and turned its ponderous head; the vast, nocturnal eyes surveyed Anasuya, saw her exactly as she was, and, accepting, closed once more in sleep. She sank against it, trembling with exhaustion and relief. It was the first time since she had left home that she had touched a non-human.

The encounter shook her deeply. It reminded her of the first time she had seen a seaphant up close, as a child. The laghori was nothing like a seaphant, but its enormous presence eased her despair a little.

The Festival lasted ninety-four days, during which it provided an easy hiding place. At night she sought shelter among the laghoris; in the day she wandered with the crowds, mingling among them like a shadow, remembering to return to the Temple of the Two Lovers for food only when she was half-faint with hunger. Sometimes Anasuya heard the peri-humans or the dour Ghoomin tribesfolk discuss the artwork displayed in the halls of the Temple of Mathematical Poetry and gathered that they were discussing her work, or the work of the person she had been. But it was like hearing about a person one had known and half-forgotten.

The news feeds were full of her disappearance. Her mates were distraught, begging for information. Searches had already been carried out by the Temple but had been thwarted during Festival time, with adolescents and others painted in green, cavorting about the plazas. Anasuya found it easier, now, to paint the few green spots on her body brown. She cut her hair short. She could truly lose herself in the great crowds and noise that disturbed for a time, the normal functioning of the City.

The day came when the last green patch on her skin (on her left temple) gave way to the invasion of brown. Now there was no need for paint at all...

She was tired. She looked back at her life and thought of all the energy that had gone into creating and riding. All that passion, spent. She had been so young, then, and she was still young in years, but she felt old.

What distracted her from her grief was a violent perturbation of her bowels. She had been feeling a little sick for the past few days but hadn't really noticed it. It was only when she lay in a laghori pen, doubled up with pain that it occurred to her that the dying of her athmis might affect the rest of her body chemistry. She staggered to the nearest public latrine, where she got relief for a few hours. It was hard to huddle in the dirt near the latrine, in the darkness outside the pool of light cast by the floating lanterns; it was hard to see people, shadowy in the night, passing by, talking, laughing, while she waited with a bitter taste in her mouth for the next spasm. If a stranger hadn't given her water, she might have died right there. The stranger, a dour Ghoomin woman who was as unlike Silaf as could be imagined, half-dragged her to a dark, smelly tent where an old man dispensed medication. She almost gagged on the pungent herbal paste they made her swallow, but once it went down it stayed down. She spent the next two days in a tent in an exhausted sleep. When she woke up, her Ghoomin benefactor was ladling her a stew, something bland and sticky. She found, to her surprise, that she could eat. Tears of gratitude sprang to her eyes. The woman, tall, bony and gaunt-eyed, nodded at her in a grim, satisfied way.

So she spent the rest of the Festival season wandering, hiding, camping with the Ghoomin or the laghori herd.

One day the peri-humans began to pack up their goods in preparation for the long journey across the continent. The Ghoomin now broke into three separate streams, having made their bargains, sealed nuptial agreements, and properly cremated their dead. The plazas were filled with the loud, horn-like baying of the laghoris, the barking laughter of the peri-humans, and the wild cries of the gwi as they flew overhead. Once they left, the City would settle down to its customary quiet and order; the hot dry smell of sand and machinery would dull the strong odors of the camps. Anasuya thought she wouldn't be able to bear it.

That day she found herself climbing up the steps of the Temple of Mathematical Arts, under the great statue of Anhutip. The Temple seemed so enormous and strange, she could not imagine that she had spent so many years of her life here. She joined the crowds that were admiring the holos that she had created. A new doorkeeper—a thin man with an obsidian faceplate whom she had never seen before—was explaining to the awed throng that this was the work of the great Anasuya, the Mathematical Poet who had disappeared. Acolyte guides explained her work: "Notice this Invonic function here, and this beautiful melding with a choric harmony of the first order…"

Her eyes filled with tears. It was beautiful, what she had done. Even if she didn't understand it any more, it was beautiful. She had never before seen her work from this distance, like just another spectator. She stood and stared at her last holo until the crowds thinned and she was the only one standing there, a slight brown woman in a white robe.

"Time to leave—we close for mid-day," the doorkeeper said, not impolitely. He was anxious to finish his duties. She let him usher her into the afternoon light. Behind her the door closed with a tremendous, echoing finality.

She went down the stairs and crossed the little plaza. In the larger plaza beyond, the peri-humans were folding their tents and loading the laghoris. She went up to one great beast and leaned against its broad flank, digging her fingers into the matted fur and combing it the way the laghori liked. The animal rumbled with pleasure; the peri-human attending to it gave her a long, toothed grin, and said something in another tongue. She said her goodbye to the laghori and its attendant, feeling bereft. The gwi had already left, making their traditional three circles around the city before flying in formation toward the East.

At the end of the plaza there was a pale person standing as though waiting for her.

Palanik? She saw him and did not see him. He was a shadow of Palanik, a stranger, an unknown creature mocking the man she knew. But he recognized her. His eyes widened, but he knew her.

"Come home, Anasuya," he said.

"How…"

"I've heard about this…condition," he said, "in my travels. I thought if there was anything that could keep you from home, it would be something like this. Dear one, come home!"

"I've lost everything."

"Not everything," he told her, drawing her to him. His lack of comprehension hurt her.

Because she did not know what else to do, she let him lead her to the House. Here again everything was strange. The strangers who had once been her mates surrounded her, pulled her into their arms.

"Oh, Ana-love, where have you been?"

"We've been searching and searching…"

"You should have told us…you should have let yourself need us…"

"…you never know, maybe it will come back…a rest cure…you could have let us…"

The words ran into one another and became meaningless. She could not speak. Finally they stepped back from her, looking at her. She saw what she had been afraid of: that Parul was not Parul, nor was Marko as she had known him. They seemed stripped bare of something essential. She could not find the familiar comfort that their presence had once afforded her.

Distances

She stood uncertainly in the common-room, looking about her as though she had never been in this house before. The white arches, the stalactites, made her feel she was inside the skeleton of some great, dead animal. One of the holos she had brought home was still there, hanging from a long string, washing the room with waves of colored light. The others began talking again, trying to plead and cajole her out of the tremendous silence in which she was trapped. Then it came to her that Lost Silaf was not there.

"Where…?"

"She left with the gwi," Palanik said, and there were tears in his eyes. She realized then that he had been trying to tell her that for a while. "She met the family of her lover, and they are going to take the bones to the place where his ancestors' bones lie, atop some mountain. She's following them on foot. She's not alone, there are Ghoomin tribesmen traveling with her part of the way."

"She'll be all right." Marko put his arm around Parul's shoulders. "They'll know to be careful. Besides, she is Ghoomin. You know what they say, there's water even in the desert. She'll survive. She may even be back next year."

"She left that," Palanik said. He pointed. On a white ledge, high in the wall, empty eye sockets looked at her. The skull of Silaf's gwi lover. She remembered some half-forgotten lore about the gwi, that they kept the skulls of loved ones for remembrance. For a moment Silaf seemed to gaze at her from the holes in the skull.

Silaf's gift, Anasuya thought, and then, inexplicably: she left that for me.

Now Marko and Palanik were trying to comfort Parul, who was in tears. How broken they all are, Anasuya thought, like a bead necklace that has come apart. She saw then that Silaf had been what kept the pentad together, by her caring, her strangeness, her need to be part of something. And the way she took pieces of things, like the bones of her gwi lover, and tried to make them whole — not static but dynamic, ever changing: one day a sculpture, then a musical instrument, then a wind-teller — the attempt itself achieving what was otherwise impossible. Connections in time as well as space. The pentad that had not been broken by Anasuya's neglect was in pieces with Silaf's departure, and now they were all looking at her, Anasuya, as though she could put it back together for them. Why were they looking at her? They didn't even look real. She couldn't fix what was missing in them. She couldn't do anything any more. She couldn't create, or mend, or make. She made an inarticulate sound of anguish, turned, and ran out of the house into the dry heat of the afternoon, ignoring their calls. She kept running until she reached a speeder docked at a station and hopped on without knowing where it was taking her.

The sun was setting over the mesas, and lights were pricking out of the darkness, rippling over the buildings. She wandered through the plazas, taking one speeder or walkway, then another. Passing the Temple of the Lovers, she accepted without comprehension the gift of a meal from the priest who was ladling out stew to strangers as part of the evening ritual. "May you be united with your lovers," the priest said to her, and to the person behind her, and to all the hungry crowd. She leaned against a pillar with the bowl warm in her hands and stared at the great stone images of Ekatip and Shunyatip, the Lovers gazing into Time in opposite directions. Her mind felt jagged and broken, pieces of thoughts and impressions floating into her consciousness like chopped up geometries. May you be united with your lovers, the priest was saying still. She thought about Vara, and Hasha, and Lata. Sagara, the place she could never return to, because even if it was the same as when she'd left it, she wasn't the same person she'd been. A brown woman among green people. A green fish in every pool, Kzoric had said, before she died. An amnion on every planet.... Ships going faster than light, through the hyperspatial pathways that she had mapped. Her blood ran suddenly cold.

She saw then what she had done, in its fullness. Opened not only the doors of heaven, but the gateways to the children of the sea. She would have to go down there, to warn Sagara's people, to tell them she had flung the stars down into the water. She thought of Hasha's body out there somewhere, in the desert, his beautiful long bones making a ripple, a dimple in the sand. If he was alive somewhere, would he have lost his athmis too, by now? And losing it, what doors would he have opened? She shuddered, because she could not imagine him like that, alive but without the fire in his eyes. Lie in the desert sands, my love, she told him. Her throat caught. She finished her stew, spilling some of it over her tunic.

She spent that night in one of the common-houses behind the temple. In the cold stone room that was barely large enough for the bed, she fell into an exhausted sleep. If she dreamed she did not know it.

She was woken in the early hours before dawn by a commotion. The brief annual rain of the desert had come — it was late this year — and there were people shouting and the sound of running footsteps. She gathered her robe around her and wandered out into the moist, misty pre-dawn, staring about her in a bewildered manner, shading her eyes from the rain. It was still dark, except for a faint luminosity over the western mesas. The mesas and made-houses were ghosts in the mist. Still, it was a teaser of a rainstorm, lasting only a few minutes, making the crowds in the street shout with frustration when it stopped. But she went into the plaza before the Temple and saw how the rain had collected in little pools and was even now running in rivulets in the cracks between the stones. She looked up at the Lovers, Ekatip and Shunyatip, and saw, in the lamp-light, the rain-tracks on their cheeks, the rain dripping off their noses.

"Look!" a stranger said, nudging her, and she followed the boy's gaze to the pool of water at her feet, all fractured by the flagstones. The boy was entranced at his reflection. She saw herself gazing up from the water, a brown face with dark eyes, mobile, broken in pieces, mingling with the reflections of other people around her. Her hair streamed from her face, a black cloud, silver-edged in the light. Lights danced off the water, making patterns, sculpting forms, illusions. In that vast, flickering collage, arising from the multiple images, between the ripples and disturbances, she saw, at last, Vara.

She pulled her damp robe around her. There was Palanik, walking across the plaza toward her. He came up to her and they looked at each other in silence.

"One plus one is two," she told him. "The solution of a first order Kormeric equation is…"

She stopped. She remembered the formula, but she would now no longer know it any other way. A blind woman, tapping the contours of the world with a stick.

"My poem is incomplete," she said, letting her tears run down her cheeks.

He nodded. He held out his hand. The Temple plaza was on a rise; she saw the City spread before her, a maze of lights in the pale dawn. There was the walkway that led to the House. She saw it go between made-houses, intersect other walkways, saw again and for the first time the path home. Why hadn't she thought of simply turning around? The path home was never a straight line: there was the House, the seaweed forest, the embrace of her mates, the leviathans calling her lost soul home.

She took a deep breath, and in its moist aroma at last was the promise of the sea. She had to go home to warn her people, but even without all that had happened, she would have had to return to Sagara. She knew that now. Her breath caught with longing. But the path home would take her first to the House, with Palanik, where she could finally learn the things she hadn't had time to learn before. She had a lead time of fourteen years, after all.

She took Palanik's hand. In the west the sun was rising, the stars were going out slowly. The stars would never be the same again; she and Nirx had made sure of that. She could hear the faint baying of the laghoris as a caravan passed somewhere not far from her. There were the lanterns floating in the half-dark. Ahead of them, the City lay like a luminous flower, lights turning out to greet the dawn. The House was somewhere there, in the distance. They turned their steps toward it.

Credit Card Purchase of Multiple Lens
Literary Guillotine
204 Locust St.
Santa Cruz, CA 95060
(831) 457-1195

2/25/2014 1:55:18 PM Invoice # 175081
Cashier ID: JJV
Sharon ID: 2
# of Items: 1

Discounted
1835500842   1 @ $12.00 $12.00

Sub Total $12.00
Tax A Total $1.01
Grand Total $13.01

```
Credit Card Purchase -- Multiple Cards
        Literary Guillotine
          204 Locust St.
        Santa Cruz, CA  95060
          (831) 457-1195


2/28/2014 1:32:18 PM   Invoice # 193081
Cashier ID:  01
Station ID:  2
# of items:  1
=========================================
Distances
1933500263    1 @       $12.00    $12.00
=========================================
Sub Total                         $12.00
Tax 1 Total                        $1.05
Grand Total                       $13.05
```

Distances

Biography

Vandana Singh was born and raised in New Delhi, India, and currently lives in the United States with her husband, daughter, and dog. Her science fiction and fantasy short fiction has been published in numerous venues, including the anthologies *Polyphony* (Volumes 1 and 3) and *Interfictions*, and the zine *Strange Horizons*. Her most recent publication is a novelette in the anthology *Clockwork Phoenix*, edited by Mike Allen. Meanwhile the last novella she published with Aqueduct, *Of Love and Other Monsters*, was reprinted in 2008 in *The Year's Best Science Fiction*, Vol. 25, edited by Gardner Dozois. For more about her, please see her website at http://users.rcn.com/singhvan.